# STAR TREK®
## THE AMAZING STORIES

# STAR TREK®
# THE AMAZING STORIES

by

M. Shayne Bell
John Gregory Betancourt
Greg Cox
A. C. Crispin
Christie Golden
Josepha Sherman and Susan Shwartz
D. W. "Prof" Smith

POCKET BOOKS
New York   London   Toronto   Sydney   Singapore

An *Original* Publication of POCKET BOOKS

POCKET BOOKS, a division of Simon & Schuster, Inc.
1230 Avenue of the Americas, New York, NY 10020

This book is published by Pocket Books, a division of Simon & Schuster, Inc., under exclusive license from Paramount Pictures.

ISBN: 0-7434-4915-0

First Pocket Books trade paperback printing August 2002

10  9  8  7  6  5  4  3  2  1

POCKET and colophon are registered trademarks of Simon & Schuster, Inc.

For information regarding special discounts for bulk purchases, please contact Simon & Schuster Special Sales at 1-800-456-6798 or business@simonandschuster.com

Printed in the U.S.A.

# Contents

**STAR TREK**
**THE NEXT GENERATION**®

**STAR TREK**
**VOYAGER**®

# Last Words

## By A. C. Crispin

Amanda's garden was still beautiful.

He stood there staring at it, surprised to discover that it was still maintained. As far as he knew, Spock had not lived in the house for some time. But the garden had been cared for . . . the spiky black blossoms were properly trimmed, the scarlet wax-leafed bushes pruned, the green waterstone paths raked, the rock arrangements stacked precisely. . . .

He wandered down the paths, hands tucked into the sleeves of his long desert robe, his nostrils taking in the exotic scents of desert plants from a dozen worlds.

Leaving Amanda's garden, he began walking toward distant Vulcan's Forge, pleased by his effortless strides. Information filled his mind, neatly cataloged, and his conclusions were, once again—it had been so long!—faultlessly logical.

The desert surrounded him now as he walked tirelessly, his

strong young body obeying his every wish. *Youth is wasted on the young* . . . he thought, remembering an ancient human saying. Well, for once humans were completely correct.

His mind was so clear, his thinking so precise. Emotion was, once more, suppressed. How agreeable to be able to think clearly, to be free of the constant, degrading assault of emotion!

For a moment it occurred to him to wonder where he was going, and why, but he resolutely suppressed that question. It was enough to be clearheaded and strong of body once more. It was enough to be traveling, going. . . .

Going where?

Once again, he repressed that question, repressed it sternly. *Where is not important. What is important is that I have regained my logic, my control. What is important is that I feel young again . . . strong again. . . .*

He looked up at the reddish sky, and beheld with wonder a wind-rider gliding along the thermals. Such a fragile, nearly translucent creature—how could it survive Vulcan's hot winds?

But survive it did . . . and he was fortunate indeed to see it. He had been alive a very long time indeed, and had only seen a handful of wind-riders in all that time. . . .

Alive . . . *was* he alive?

Such a question was not logical, and he repressed it, also. Enough to walk, to be clear of mind, controlled, strong and alert. Enough to—

"*Captain. Captain Picard. Wake up.*"

His surroundings shimmered, faded. No! He was on Vulcan, he was in control, he was walking, going—

"*Captain Picard. You directed that you wished to be awakened at oh-seven-hundred hours. Wake up, please.*"

The sleeper's eyes opened. Vulcan vanished. He blinked, dazed and confused. His surroundings were . . . unfamiliar. Softly gleaming walls; clean-lined, functional furnishings. Not Vulcan in style. Human. He recognized them. He had, after all, had two human wives.

*Amanda?* he thought, but then he remembered. Amanda was dead. Had been dead. Perrin. Perrin was his wife.

"Perrin?" he whispered.

His voice was completely unfamiliar. He blinked and sat up. *What is happening?* Apprehension stirred, but he repressed it sternly, as was proper.

Rising, he strode over to the washstand. The mirror above it reflected an image. A human male, middle-aged, bald, with handsome, aristocratic features. He recognized that face.

*Jean-Luc Picard.*

He blinked, and the image blinked back.

Suddenly the world shifted, tilted, and the last of the dream images fled. He gasped, swayed, and instinctively grabbed the washstand to steady himself. He closed his eyes, and when he opened them again, the room steadied. Reality rushed back.

Captain Jean-Luc Picard stared at himself in the mirror. *In my dream, I was Sarek. Young again, in control again, strong and logical. . . .* Slowly, Picard ran water into the basin, then splashed it onto his face. The cool liquid felt refreshing against his skin. Reaching for a towel, he wiped his face.

*I haven't dreamed that I was Sarek for months. Why now? It's so ironic that I should dream of our mind-meld now, because Sarek is, after all, dead. He died four days ago, at home on Vulcan. His memorial service is scheduled for tomorrow. . . .*

Picard walked over to a chair, lowered himself into it. His previous dreams about Sarek had been fuzzy, distorted, shadows left over from the mind-meld they had shared. Nothing akin to what he'd just experienced. That had been so clear, so *real!* He'd awakened actually believing himself to *be* Sarek. But the Vulcan Ambassador was dead. Bendii Syndrome had killed him, after a lingering last illness that had left Sarek stripped of all emotional control. A cruel disease, Bendii Syndrome. Picard couldn't imag-

5

ine a worse fate for a Vulcan than losing all emotional control, having his feelings bared for anyone to witness.

*Why now?* Picard thought. Then the events of yesterday came rushing back, and he knew.

Yesterday, Picard had left Ambassador Spock behind on Romulus to continue his efforts to reunite the Romulan and Vulcan peoples. After Spock had told Picard of his decision to remain on Romulus, Picard had bade the Vulcan a reluctant farewell.

But, as a last gesture of goodwill, the captain had invited Spock to mind-meld with him. Spock and Sarek, the Vulcan had admitted, had never chosen to meld, so Picard made the offer so Spock could experience Sarek's mind through him.

As Spock had sensed Sarek's consciousness from the captain's mind, his Vulcan control had visibly faltered, and it was obvious Spock was finally allowing himself to grieve over the loss of his father.

Picard had been glad to be able to give the Vulcan that last chance at contact with Sarek. . . .

*The mind-meld with Ambassador Spock,* Picard realized. *It must have awakened the part of me that was linked to Sarek during our meld. That explains that vivid dream. . . .*

Picard glanced over at his replicator. "Tea, Earl Grey, hot," he said. His voice was steady. It was only a dream, after all.

The captain sipped his tea while he dressed, and his mind drifted back to the last few minutes he had spent with Spock the day before. As they walked along the ancient Romulan passage from the meeting place, Spock had glanced over at Picard and said, "Thank you for bringing me the news of my father's death, Picard. I have thought about him a great deal over the past few days."

"As have I," Picard had responded. "If we can return to Federation space in time, I intend to request that the *Enterprise* be sent to Vulcan. I would like to attend Sarek's memorial service."

6

"Yes," Spock replied. "It would be only proper to have the flagship of the Federation in attendance. And her captain, of course."

*Sarek's memorial service* . . . thought the captain. *I must contact the admiral.*

After checking on the bridge and going through the usual morning status reports, Picard retired to his ready room and activated the communications relay.

Only a minute later, the captain found himself looking at the image of Admiral Brackett, the Starfleet officer who had sent him to find Ambassador Spock on Romulus and determine whether the Vulcan had—as Starfleet feared—defected.

Brackett blinked at the captain of the *Enterprise* in surprise. "Captain! This is pleasant, if unexpected. Do you have something to add to your report?"

Picard shook his head, feeling bemused, but then found himself speaking in his usual precise, assured tones. "Admiral, Ambassador Sarek's memorial service is tomorrow. I request that the *Enterprise* be permitted to represent Starfleet there."

Brackett hesitated, then said, "I have assigned the *Potemkin,* Captain."

Picard's lips tightened. "But, Admiral, if I may—"

Her rounded features beneath her short hair softened as the admiral interrupted. "Jean-Luc, I know you and Ambassador Sarek were . . . close. If you wish to attend, I will authorize the *Enterprise* to serve as a second honor guard vessel. Goodness knows, a man of Sarek's stature deserves to have the flagship of the fleet in attendance. Can you make it there in time? It will be tight."

Picard nodded, and a tremendous feeling of relief swept through him. He would be there, as he *must* be. He would be able to say a final farewell to the Vulcan he had shared minds with. Admiral Brackett was correct—he and Sarek had been as close as it was possible for two sentient beings to be. They had, for the duration of the Legaran negotiations, become one mind, one consciousness.

7

"The *Enterprise* will be there, Admiral," Picard said. "And I thank you."

She nodded. "Pity Ambassador Spock won't be in attendance. It's traditional, I understand, for the family members of the deceased to make a brief statement." Brackett regarded Picard across the parsecs. "I read your report, Captain. Talk about what you call 'cowboy diplomacy'! Tell me . . . do you think Spock has a snowball's chance in hell of fostering reunification between the Romulans and the Vulcans?"

Picard shook his head. "I don't know, Admiral. I do know that he is determined to try, and that there is no one better suited to the task."

She nodded. "Again, Captain, I commend you and your crew for the excellent work on uncovering that Romulan plot. If it hadn't been for the *Enterprise,* Vulcan might actually have been in danger of finding itself occupied by a Romulan invasion force."

"I believe that Sela and the Proconsul gravely underestimated the spirit of the Vulcan people, Admiral," Picard said. "Being a pacifist is by no means the same thing as being weak. If that Romulan force had actually landed on Vulcan, they would have been dealt with . . . logically and efficiently."

Brackett smiled, her small eyes dancing. "I think you're right, Jean-Luc."

After Picard broke the connection, he walked onto the bridge, to find Commander Data at the helm. "Mr. Data, set course for Vulcan," he said.

Data's fingers were a blur over the navigational controls. "Course laid in, Captain."

"Ahead warp factor seven, Mr. Data. Engage."

The *Enterprise* quivered fractionally; then the star-blurs surrounding them narrowed and elongated even more as the great starship flung herself into high warp.

\* \* \*

8

As the merciless Vulcan sun hovered above the distant, rugged horizon, Captain Picard, Lieutenant Commander La Forge, and Commander Data materialized not far from the ancient steps that zigzagged up the peak known as Mount Seleya.

Midway up the mountain stood the temple and amphitheater where Sarek's memorial service would be held. Memorials were traditionally held at sunset, but a few early arrivals were already there, long Vulcan robes brushing the ground, their sandaled feet flashing from beneath their folds as they began the ascent.

Picard took a deep breath of the thin air, feeling the heat strike him like a blow. Even with forty Eridani no longer directly overhead, it was like standing before a roaring bonfire. The heat enveloped him like a lover, clinging to every centimeter of skin, and the thin air didn't help. Picard was grateful for the dose of tri-ox Beverly Crusher had administered to the two humans before permitting them to beam down.

The captain stood there, gazing around him, feeling an odd sense of having *come home.*

But he had only been on Vulcan a few times in his life, most recently just a week ago, when he had gone to visit Sarek during his last days. Picard had beamed down to the front steps of Sarek's home in ShiKahr, and gotten only a brief glimpse of the ambassador's home as Perrin had guided him to Sarek's stark, unadorned bedroom. It had distressed the captain greatly to see the ambassador reduced to a shivering, babbling shell of the man Picard had admired for years—admired even before he'd ever met him.

Moved by an impulse he didn't stop to analyze, Picard turned away from the steps, and stared down at the plains below. There, in the middle of the flat land, lay the city of ShiKahr.

As Picard stood there, looking down on ShiKahr, memories not his own assailed him. He realized that he *knew* ShiKahr, knew it as well as he knew the family vineyards back on Earth in the French province of Lombardy. He could have been set down anywhere in the city below and unerringly made his way around, finding shops, public gathering places, the homes of Sarek's friends and colleagues. The captain of the *Enterprise* realized that he could have walked unerringly from one end of the city to the other.

A benefit of sharing Sarek's mind last year. . . .

*But that was a year ago,* Picard thought. *Why am I experiencing these memories now?*

It wasn't just memories of places; there were memories of people he'd never known, too. When he'd first regarded Ambassador Spock's saturnine features a few days ago on Romulus, Picard had experienced a flicker of recognition and joy at seeing his best friend once more. There was just one catch—at the time when they met on Romulus, Picard barely knew Ambassador Spock, except by reputation. He had met him only once, decades before, when he'd attended Spock's bonding ceremony—as someone had explained it, "more than a betrothal, but somewhat less than a formal marriage, Lieutenant."

So why that instant of joyful recognition? That spark of emotion one feels for one's closest friend?

It had taken Picard some time to sort out, but finally he'd been able to identify those emotions. Apparently Sarek had also mind-melded with another captain of the *Enterprise,* some time before Captain James T. Kirk's tragic death back in 2293. Kirk had died a hero while saving the *Enterprise*-B from some kind of strange space anomaly. He was one of Starfleet and the Federation's greatest heroes. And he and Spock had been best friends.

Picard wondered why he wasn't experiencing anger at Sarek for leaving him with these grafted-on memories. After the Borg "possession" of his body and mind had transformed him into Locutus, he'd been so filled with rage, hatred, and anger that it had sickened him, and he'd considered leaving Starfleet. It had taken him a visit to Earth and Labarre, plus many sessions with Counselor Troi, before he'd been able to sleep without terrifying nightmares.

But the meld with Sarek, while it had left him with memories not his own, just wasn't the same. Even now, after experiencing the occasionally unsettling and inconvenient flashes from that other mind, Picard was still glad that he'd chosen to meld with Sarek.

Picard slowly turned away from his home (*His* home? No! Sarek's home! Spock's home! Not his!) and let himself take in the stark, terrifying beauty of the landscape before him.

Jagged stone thrust upward like spears. The lowering sun turned the naked rockfaces the color of human blood. Two peaks challenged the sky—Mount Seleya was the taller of the two by far; a narrow stone bridge connected it to the slender spire that was Mount Trenaya. Even though Picard didn't speak Vulcan, he discovered that he knew the meanings of those names. "Seleya" meant "sacred mountain" and "Trenaya" meant "infant mountain."

Since time out of mind, Mount Seleya had housed the adepts of the Vulcan mental disciplines. Much of the mountain was honeycombed with chambers, corridors, and shrines cut from the living rock. It was here, in the Hall of Ancient Thought, that the *katras* of those who had passed on paused and took their final, incorporeal, leave-taking before departing for What Lay Ahead.

When a Vulcan lay dying, he or she would be brought here, and the adepts would help ease the transition of the *katra* from the body to the Hall of Ancient Thought.

*Except in Spock's case,* Picard thought. It was one of the strangest chapters in Ambassador Spock's extraordinary record that his empty but still-breathing shell had once been brought here by Captain Kirk and his friends, and his mind and spirit had been re-fused in an ancient ritual known as *fal-tor-pan.*

"Wow," Geordi La Forge said. "This is my first time on Vulcan, Captain." He wiped his forehead with the sleeve of his uniform. "Even hotter than I expected, but it's worth it. What an incredible view I'm seeing! The different heat signatures make everything shimmer in bands of color."

The chief engineer turned his VISORed head, studying the ever-increasing tide of people who were passing through the security checkpoint, then heading for the steps. "That's going to be quite a hike, Captain, especially in this thin air," he added. "Too bad we have to walk up. If I'd known it was this steep, I'd have had O'Brien beam us to the summit."

Picard shook his head. "No," he said, and his voice was harsh, unfamiliar to his own ears. "It is traditional to walk."

"Indeed," Data said, "the ascension of Mount Seleya is analogous, in Vulcan spiritual tradition, to the journey made by the soul in many human cultures. The physical ascent is supposed to cleanse the body and spirit of worldly ties, much as the crossing of the River Jordan, the Styx, the sword-bridge to Raganarok, the—"

Picard turned to regard his android officer, his "now is not the time for a lecture" look in place. Data broke off and subsided.

"Time for us to start," Picard said. "Starfleet has cautioned me that the Vulcans have refused to have heavy security, only this one checkpoint to verify that all attending are unarmed. So we must all remain alert for any problems. Sarek's memorial service has brought some of the highest officials in the Federation here to pay their last respects. Even the President of the Federation is scheduled to attend. She will be accompanied by security, but many other dignitaries—especially Vulcan ones—will not."

Picard glanced up at the peak. "Admiral Brackett informed me that even the Legarans have sent a delegation to honor the man who helped them negotiate formal ties to the Federation."

Geordi La Forge wiped his forehead again. "Well, the Legarans ought to like it here. It's fifty-one-point-six degrees at the moment, and they only need another hundred degrees to make their tank just to their liking."

Picard nodded. Nobody knew more about the Legarans' requirements for life support than La Forge. It had been the chief engineer's unenviable duty to prepare the tank of bubbling, varicolored slime for the Legarans during Sarek's last negotiation.

"Cheer up, Geordi," Data said. "As is typical of desert environments, the temperature should decline rapidly after sunset."

"Yeah, by that time we'll be gone," La Forge said. "Or I'll have melted into a puddle of goo myself."

"Let's go," Picard said. Shoulder to shoulder, the three Starfleet officers walked forward, passed through the security scan, and began climbing the ancient steps.

The steps themselves were carved deeply into the rock, but generations upon generations of Vulcan feet had worn them, made them slightly uneven. Picard, who was on the outside of the steps, had to watch his footing, because there was no railing. He resisted the urge to look over the increasingly precipitous dropoff that yawned to his left.

Twice during the ascent the captain signaled a break so he and La Forge could catch their breath. Both officers were in excellent physical shape, but the heat and the thin air were taking a toll. Each time, they had to step aside to allow Vulcans to pass them. Even the oldest of the Vulcans climbed tirelessly and without pause. Picard was reminded forcibly of Vulcan superior strength.

*Yes, indeed,* he thought, recalling his conversation with Admiral Brackett, *the Romulan invasion force would have had its hands full with these people. . . .*

He found himself wishing that Ambassador Spock had accompanied him back to Vulcan, even briefly, to attend the service, but he knew that the danger of crossing the Neutral Zone made that notion impossible. Still, it would have meant a lot to Sarek to have his son present today.

Thinking of Spock's stormy relationship with Sarek made Picard recall his own father, dead now many years. He and Maurice had never gotten along, either. Picard's father had strongly disapproved of Starfleet and all advanced technology. He'd wanted his son, Jean-Luc, to stay home in Labarre and tend the family vine-yards. He'd been quite vocal in his displeasure when Jean-Luc had disobeyed him and entered Starfleet Academy.

Picard frowned as he pushed himself to keep climbing. Last year, he'd had a very strange vision when his artificial heart had failed, and he'd actually "died" for a few minutes, until Beverly had managed to resuscitate him. During his "death" he'd imag-ined that Q was there in the afterlife, tormenting him. Q had pro-duced an image of Maurice Picard, and once again Jean-Luc had been forced to relive how he'd disappointed his father.

Even after all those years, remembering the day he'd told his fa-ther of his decision still had the power to make Jean-Luc Picard's jaw clench, his mouth tighten.

*I am sorry I was a disappointment to you,* he thought, remem-bering his father's craggy features, his accusing stare. *But I made the right decision. Robert took over the vineyards, after all . . . and he resented it, all these years, he resented it. So would I have, if I had done as you wished,* mon père. . . .

Would it have done any good to explain, to try to talk to his fa-ther? Every time he'd tried to talk to Maurice after his admission to Starfleet Academy, there had just been another fight, and the gulf between them had widened still further. *Should I have tried harder? Been more patient?* Picard didn't know. *And now . . . it is too late. Death is the most final argument of all.*

Picard was wheezing for breath, and Geordi La Forge was in little better shapc, when they finally mounted the last step. Picard stepped aside and stood there, trying to catch his breath. He was drenched in sweat.

"Here, Captain, Geordi," Data said, unfastening a small case he wore on his belt. "Dr. Crusher gave me these in case they were needed." With two deft motions, the android pressed the injectors against the officers' arms.

Picard's breathing immediately eased. He smiled at Data and nodded. "Thank you, Commander. I needed that."

"Me, too," Geordi said. "Thanks, Data."

Picard and La Forge, on Crusher's advice, had each carried a small flask of water, and they paused for a moment to drink some. Then, feeling somewhat more alert, Picard gazed at the vista before them.

They were at least a thousand meters higher than when they had begun. Mount Seleya's flank had been flattened, here, and paved. Behind them, buried in the bulk of the mountain, was the Hall of Ancient Thought and the quarters of the Vulcan mental adepts.

Before them lay the gathering ground for the crowd. The immediate family, Sarek's closest friends, and the highest-ranked dignitaries would cross that slender tongue of stone to stand in the most sacred spot of all, the amphitheater. Some buried part of Sarek's memories told Picard that the amphitheater was where Spock's re-fusion had taken place, seven, almost eight decades ago.

"Where should we stand, Captain?" Data asked.

"Well, we're not part of the family," Picard said. He squinted into the setting sun. "How about over there, not far from the Legaran tank? We should be able to see the proceedings from there."

The three officers began making their way over toward the Legaran tank. Picard could see a faint shimmer above the tank and on each side, and realized that the Legarans' special environment must be protected by an energy field. Otherwise, the tank would give off so much heat that it would be like standing in an oven.

As Picard made his way through the crowd, he inadvertently brushed against one of the robed Vulcans. Knowing that Vulcans were touch-telepaths, the captain halted and turned to face the person he'd bumped. "My apologies—"

The tall young Vulcan facing him was staring at him intently, and then recognition dawned for both of them at the same time.

"Captain Picard."

"Sakkath!"

Last year, the Vulcan had accompanied Ambassador Sarek during his last mission to complete the negotiations with the Legarans. Sakkath had tried and failed to keep Sarek's uncontrolled emotions, a result of the Bendii Syndrome, in check. Violent altercations had begun erupting all over the *Enterprise* after crew members had been exposed to Sarek's inadvertent telepathic broadcasts of his raging emotions.

When a mind-meld had proved necessary to complete the negotiations, it had been Picard, with his experience in diplomacy, who had volunteered to share his mind with Sarek, to allow the Vulcan ambassador to "borrow" his own emotional control.

Now, a year later, Picard studied Sakkath, seeing that his features seemed drawn, thinner. Sakkath had aged far more than a year. "I'm glad to see you, Sakkath," Picard said, nodding to La Forge and Data and motioning the Vulcan aside so they could speak in private. "How have you been?"

The Vulcan inclined his head gravely. "I am well, Captain," he said. "I am . . . gratified that you could attend today."

"So am I," Picard said. "It seemed fitting."

"Indeed," Sakkath said. "Sarek spoke of you many times this past year, Captain, during his increasingly infrequent lucid moments. He was very grateful to you for helping him complete his final mission."

"You . . . cared . . . for Sarek during his final illness?" Picard said, marveling a little. He could only imagine how painful it would have been for a Vulcan to be constantly assaulted by Sarek's emotional storms.

"Perrin and I attended to him," Sakkath said. "It was all I could do for him to make up for my inability to help him during the Legaran mission."

"You did your best," Picard reminded him.

"But, Captain, it was *you* who mind-melded with him, not I," Sakkath said. "I should have been strong enough to do that . . . and I was not. I failed him."

"Nonsense," Picard said. "We discussed that at the time, and you would have been risking your health and sanity to undertake that meld. Humans are far more equipped to handle violent emotions than Vulcans."

"True," Sakkath admitted. He regarded Picard intently, then did something no Vulcan had ever done before in the captain's experience—he held out his hand, human-style. "I will always be grateful to you, nevertheless, Captain Picard."

Hesitantly, Jean-Luc held out his own hand, and felt the young Vulcan's hot flesh grasp his own. Vulcans had a higher body temperature than humans. Gravely, they shook hands, and, as they did so, a fleeting expression crossed the Vulcan's normally impassive features. An expression of . . . what? Recognition? Discovery? Picard couldn't be certain.

"Captain," Sakkath said in soft tones that held a note of urgency, "You must come with me. Perrin will wish to see you."

Picard realized from the direction of Sakkath's gaze that he was proposing to lead him across the bridge, to the section reserved for family and close friends. "I don't want to intrude," Picard said. "I can see her after the service."

"No," Sakkath said, and there was no mistaking the tension in his voice. "You must come, Captain. It is necessary . . . that is, proper . . . that you be there."

"Well, I . . . ." Picard hesitated. "Let me speak to my officers," he said.

Sakkath nodded, and followed him back to where Geordi and Data were waiting, not far from the Legarans' tank. "I'm sure you both recall Sakkath, Sarek's aide," Picard said, and the officers and the Vulcan exchanged greetings.

Picard explained that he was going to go and speak with Perrin, and would be back after the service. He turned away, ready to follow Sakkath, but he'd only gone a few steps when Geordi La Forge caught up to him. "Captain!"

Picard swung around. "What is it?"

17

"Sir . . . you warned us to keep an eye out for potential problems with security. . . ." Geordi said softly, keeping his voice low. "I think we have one." The Chief Engineer nodded over at a Vulcan who stood not far from them, wearing the typical homespun Vulcan robe that so many of his people favored. "Does that man over there appear to you to be a typical Vulcan?"

"Yes," Picard said. "Why?"

"Well, he's not," La Forge said, still speaking in low tones. "His temperature is three degrees cooler than the lowest temperature for a normal Vulcan."

Picard frowned. "What does that mean? That he's ill?"

"I don't think so, sir," La Forge said. "I think he's a Romulan. I've seen Romulans before, and his heat patterns match theirs exactly."

The captain knew how easily a Romulan could be altered to visually pass as a Vulcan. The two species shared a common genetic heritage, after all, and looked very similar. If Beverly Crusher could easily disguise Picard to pass as a Romulan, as she had done during the captain's latest mission, how much easier would it be to disguise a Romulan to appear as a Vulcan?

"In this crowd of Vulcans, he sticks out like a sore thumb in my VISOR," La Forge added.

"I see," Picard murmured. "A Romulan. It's difficult not to imagine he's here for some ulterior purpose. Why else would he disguise himself? He could be a saboteur or an assassin. The place is certainly rife with targets. . . ." The captain thought fast. "We need to question him, verify his identity. You and Commander Data circle around and get behind him in case he resists. Sakath and I will approach from the front. We shall accost him as quietly as possible. If he is here legitimately, he'll be able to prove it. If he's not . . ."

"Right, Captain," La Forge said, and gestured to the android.

Picard and Sakkath waited until the two officers were in position; then they moved forward purposefully. The "Vulcan" looked over, saw the Starfleet uniform coming, and turned to bolt back toward the steps.

Data and Geordi grabbed him before he had gone more than a meter or two, however. He struggled briefly, but uselessly. Data's grip was inexorable.

Sakkath motioned two of the temple guards to come over and restrain the Romulan. "Search him," Picard ordered.

Quickly, efficiently, the two officers searched the Romulan. "He is unarmed, Captain," Data said.

Picard faced the man, and his last doubts that he was an innocent Vulcan died. He stood facing them, eyes defiant, and his expression was filled with emotion that no proper Vulcan would ever have permitted. "Who are you?" the captain demanded. "Why did you come here?"

The Romulan faced him in silence. Picard glanced at Sakkath. "We must discover what his mission was," he said. "If he managed to smuggle a bomb up here . . ."

"Agreed," Sakkath said. He flexed his fingers. "I believe I can discover his intentions."

As Sakkath started purposefully toward the Romulan, the man suddenly erupted into violent motion, catching the two Vulcans holding him by surprise. Lashing out with hands and feet, he managed to pull away from the guards. They sprang after him, blocking his escape.

But escape was not his intent.

As Picard stood staring in horror, the Romulan turned, sprinted the few meters to the edge of the cliff, and leaped off. Picard was frozen with shock. The saboteur's action had been so fast, accomplished in such deadly silence, that it was as though he had never been.

Recovering himself, the captain glanced over at Sakkath, saw the Vulcan's eyes narrow with concern. "The question is, Captain, did he accomplish his mission . . . whatever it was?"

"We should evacuate the area," Picard urged.

"The ceremony will begin in just a few minutes, Captain! We cannot evacuate everyone quickly."

Picard knew the Vulcan was right. *We can beam them up,* he thought, assessing his options.

La Forge came over, looking a bit shaken. "Captain, if only I had been quicker . . ."

"We've all seen what Romulans will do to avoid capture," Picard said. "Don't blame yourself, Mr. La Forge." He glanced around at the Vulcan guards, heard Sakkath giving them orders to conduct a quick sensor sweep of the area, to make sure the Romulan had not managed to smuggle in a bomb.

"Mr. La Forge, where *exactly* was the Romulan standing when you first noticed him?"

La Forge indicated the Legaran tank. "Right over there, Captain. He—" He tensed. "Captain! I think I know what he did! The temperature of the Legarans' tank is down to one hundred twenty degrees!"

Picard, Data, and the chief engineer moved hastily through the crowd until they reached the environmental controls of the Legaran delegation's tank. Picard found himself thinking how ironic it was that these beings could actually die of hypothermia in temperatures that would boil a human alive.

Geordi pried off the panel and took a look inside at the controls. "Captain, have Lieutenant Philbas beam down with a portable energy field generator, and a heating unit, plus my tools. And we'll need Dr. Crusher to check out the Legarans themselves."

Picard nodded and tapped his combadge. "Picard to *Enterprise,*" he said crisply.

Moments later Geordi was busy, with Philbas's and Data's help, replacing the smashed environmental control unit for the Legarans' tank. Picard heard the whine of a transporter beam again, and Dr. Beverly Crusher materialized, dressed in a protective environmental suit.

Cautiously, Picard and Crusher stepped to the front of the Legarans' tank and peered in through the narrow viewing orifice in the field. Picard had never actually seen a Legaran.

The four creatures huddled together shivering in the center of the tank resembled a nightmare cross between an Earth mud puppy and a Regulan bloodworm. But they stared back at Picard with huge, anxious eyes, and he knew that, despite their appearance, these were decent people who had come to honor Sarek—and almost paid for their gesture with their lives.

"I am Captain Jean-Luc Picard. A Romulan saboteur damaged your tank's controls, but we are restoring them," Picard said, hoping they would understand him. During the negotiations aboard the *Enterprise,* the Legaran delegation had understood Standard English. "Our doctor is here, and she has prepared a hypospray for each of you that will help you until your tank is again at the proper temperature. Can you understand me?"

The foremost of the shivering beings slowly nodded its wattled, spotted and fringed head. Its jaws opened, revealing large, squarish yellow teeth. A computer-generated voice spoke. "Yes, Captain Picard. I am"—an incomprehensible hiss emerged—"Minister of State. I understand your language."

"Good, Minister," Picard said. "Hold on. We're doing our best to help."

After deactivating a portion of the protective field, Picard helped Crusher over the lip of the tank, and held his breath as the suited doctor waded through the multicolored bubbling slime. Her injector hissed four times, and the violent trembling of the four beings slowly eased.

Picard glanced over at Geordi. "We're almost done here, Captain," the chief engineer reported.

"Excellent, Mr. La Forge," Picard said, thinking that he should put the chief engineer in for a commendation. He and his VISOR had saved the Legarans' lives.

The captain helped Crusher back over the lip of the tank; then the doctor began monitoring the Legarans with her med-scanner. She nodded reassuringly at Picard, and her voice issued from inside the suit's external speaker. "Hypothermia has been averted. They should be fine in a few minutes."

"Captain Picard . . ." the Legaran minister spoke again. "You say it was a Romulan who attempted to murder us?"

"Yes," Picard said. "My chief engineer spotted him. But he chose to leap to his death rather than face interrogation."

"Why would the Romulans want to kill the Legarans?" Beverly Crusher asked.

"Because Legara IV is located in a very critical area of space." Sakkath, who had been standing there in silence, spoke up. "The planet lies midway between Cardassian space and the Romulan Neutral Zone. Legara IV is one of the primary sources for velonium, which is used in warp-core shielding. The Romulans are eager to annex Legara IV . . . but in order to do so, they would first have to drive a wedge between Legara and the Federation. The murder of their delegation at an important diplomatic function would certainly accomplish that goal."

Picard nodded at Sakkath's analysis. "And undo Sarek's ninety-three years of work," he said, feeling a surge of anger at the nameless Romulan.

"We understand," came the toneless voice of the Legaran official. "This is not the first time enemies of the Federation have sought to harm our people. And, Captain Picard . . . we thank you for your help."

"Oh, you're most welcome," Picard said. "I only regret that you experienced any discomfort."

The Legaran minister blinked his huge eyes. "And now . . . may we ask you to withdraw, Captain? Your clothing is not at all proper for conversation, and it is painful to us to converse with a being not properly attired for interspecies interaction."

Picard was taken aback, until he remembered how protocol-conscious the Legarans were. "I understand," he said. "My apologies if my attire offended you, Minister."

"Under the circumstances, we are willing to overlook it, Captain," said the being graciously.

Picard beat a hasty retreat from the tank's viewing orifice.

Sakkath touched his sleeve. "It is time for the memorial service to begin," he said. "Can your crew manage without you?"

Picard hesitated, glanced at La Forge and Data. "We're up and running again, Captain," the chief engineer said. "I'll just stay here and monitor the tank as it heats back up."

"And I'll monitor the Legarans," Crusher said. "Go, Jean-Luc. Don't keep them waiting."

"Very well," Picard said, and followed Sakkath.

They walked single file across the tongue of stone. Picard gazed out across the seemingly bottomless gulf, thinking of the Romulan, wondering what it would be like to fall . . . and fall. . . .

When they reached the amphitheater, the crowd was small. Picard saw Perrin, Sarek's human wife, almost immediately. She was standing there, wearing Vulcan garb as was her custom, a long white robe, very plain. A white coif held her blonde hair back from her features. Picard had seen her just days ago, but he was saddened to see what a difference only a few days had made. Exhaustion and grief had deepened the lines on her face, until she appeared twenty years older than the woman he had known. Picard knew from Sarek's mind that she had truly loved and revered her husband.

Sakkath led Picard up to Perrin. Her eyes widened when she saw the captain. "Jean-Luc!"

Picard took her hand, bowed over it. "Please accept my condolences, Perrin. We have all lost . . . so much."

She regarded him for a long moment, then nodded. "Yes, we have, Jean-Luc. He would be glad that you are here. Please . . . stand with us."

Picard took his place on her left side, and Sakkath stood to her right.

As the hovering sun touched the horizon, a Vulcan priest struck a huge gong. The sound reverberated out into the distance, and all conversation ceased.

A tall, stern-looking Vulcan of middle years walked out into the center of the amphitheater, flanked by two acolytes. Picard realized this must be the current High Master. His voice rang out into the stillness. "Today we honor the memory of Sarek of Vulcan, son of Skon, grandson of Solkar. Sarek served our world capably for his entire adult life. We respect and honor him today as one who helped Vulcan forge strong ties with the Federation. The President of the Federation has asked to be allowed to speak, and I call upon her at this time."

The Federation President, a Tellarite female, stepped forward. "Sarek of Vulcan. What can we say about this person? He was a strong friend, an obdurate foe, and a champion of galactic peace. Today we are all the poorer for his loss. I will miss him, miss our clashes as well as our unity. Madame Sarek, in the words of your adopted people . . . today I grieve with thee."

The High Master nodded at the Federation President, then at Perrin. "It is time for the family members to speak."

Perrin took a step forward. "I am all the family that Sarek had left," she said, her voice husky, but strong. She spoke in English, but her speech patterns had a Vulcan cadence to them. "Sarek's son chose to forsake his father and forsake Vulcan . . . because, as you can all see, Spock is not here today."

Picard remembered that Perrin and Spock had never gotten along. Perrin felt that Spock's political views during the Cardassian conflicts had constituted a betrayal of his father. "I am very protective of my husband, Captain," she'd said once. "I do not apologize for it."

The captain took a deep breath, feeling rather light-headed. *I must need another dose of tri-ox,* he thought.

24

Perrin fell silent, obviously struggling for control. All those years on Vulcan had taught her something, because, a moment later, she spoke again, her voice shaking but understandable. "My husband was a great man, and we will never again see his like. The galaxy has lost . . . much. I miss him, and I mourn him . . . I will always mourn him. Grieve with me, my friends, for Sarek is . . . gone."

She made a slight, all-inclusive gesture, then bowed her head.

Picard blinked in confusion, realizing that he had taken a step forward so that he again stood shoulder to shoulder with Perrin. She glanced over at him, plainly surprised. The captain felt his mouth opening, heard himself speak in a voice that was not his own—*in fluent Vulcan.*

The faces of the crowd registered surprise and, in Perrin's case, utter shock.

Even though Picard did not understand or speak Vulcan, the words he was speaking resonated within him, and he knew their meaning:

"Greetings. I am Spock, son of Sarek, grandson of Skon. My words come from the mouth of my father's and my friend, Captain Picard of the starship *Enterprise.* It is not possible for me to be with you today to honor my father. I am far away on a mission to promote galactic peace. My mission honors my father's memory. Sarek and I often did not agree. Everyone knows that. And yet . . . he is the reason I am where I am today."

Even as Picard spoke, the words coming readily to his lips, his mind flashed back to the last moments of the meld with Spock. Now he recalled the Vulcan's unspoken question and his own wordless assent: Spock's final message had been implanted on such a deep subconscious level that it had stayed buried in his mind until the proper moment.

Even the normally stoic Vulcans reacted visibly to Picard's words, with varying degrees of surprise. Perrin was staring at Picard, shock and anger plain on her aristocratic features.

Picard realized that the crowd was hearing him speak in

Spock's voice. *He wanted to be here, but knew it was impossible. So he chose the only way to speak at his father's memorial. . . .*

"I honor my father. In life, I respected him. Sarek taught me a great deal. He taught me to revere Infinite Diversity In Infinite Combinations. He taught me that peace was the best way. He taught me to be strong, to face my duty unswervingly . . . and that is what I am doing."

Picard took a deep breath, realizing his mouth and throat felt strange from shaping those alien words.

"I do not know if I shall ever be able to return to Vulcan. I am working for peace, teaching the Vulcan way . . . the way of Surak. The way of Sarek."

Picard felt tears sting his eyes as Spock's words made him remember his own conflicts with his father. "Goodbye, my father. Your struggle is over. May you find peace where you are, and may I help bring about peace where I am. I shall miss you always, and I grieve that you and I will never look upon each other again. Farewell, Sarek."

Picard fell silent.

Perrin gazed at the captain, and Picard could tell that she was angry—whether at him or at Spock, he could not say.

Then Sakkath stepped forward. "As the Keeper of the *Katra,* I have climbed the steps of Mount Seleya. I have listened to the words of Sarek's wife . . . and of his son. I shall now convey Sarek's *katra* to the Hall of Ancient Thought, for his final leave-taking." The ambassador's aide inclined his head slightly, first to Perrin, then to Picard.

Then the young Vulcan turned and walked away, and the crowd of mourners parted before him as he headed out onto the narrow stone bridge.

*He knew,* Picard realized. *When Sakkath touched me, somehow he knew, even though I did not, that I was carrying Spock's final message to Sarek. That is why he insisted I stand with the family. . . .*

Picard took a deep breath, and then another as he watched the young Vulcan's tall form dwindle away in the gathering darkness. *Fathers and sons* . . . the captain thought. *Did Sarek, at last, finally understand his son? Did my father at some point understand—and forgive—me?*

Jean-Luc Picard knew he would never know. And yet . . . for some reason he felt encouraged, buoyed. A cooling breeze touched his cheek, and he felt at peace.

Night descended upon Vulcan, a night full of stars.

# Bedside Matters

## By Greg Cox

"Dammit, I'm a doctor, not a veterinarian!"

Beverly Crusher sighed and rolled her eyes, none too surprised by the familiar grousing of the *Enterprise*'s Emergency Medical Hologram. This wasn't the first time the EMH had gotten on her nerves; for an artificial lifeform, the holographic doctor had a markedly abrasive personality, not to mention a highly questionable bedside manner.

*I'd just as soon not use the darn thing at all,* she thought, *except in the most extreme emergencies, but Starfleet Medical keeps pestering me for evaluation reports on this wonderful new technological innovation.*

Ironically, it was Crusher herself who had approved the initial funding and development of the EMH project, back during her yearlong stint as head of Starfleet Medical. *It seemed like a good idea at the time,* she reflected wryly.

Right now, however, the hologram was a mass of fuming photons, characteristically indignant at the simple task for which Crusher had activated him. "I'm programmed with over five million possible treatments," the EMH protested, his arms crossed atop his chest as he confronted Beverly in sickbay, "along with the accumulated knowledge and diagnostic capabilities of two thousand medical references, forty-seven physicians, and over three thousand humanoid cultures, and to what crucial medical challenge is the sum total of this awesome amount of expertise applied to? Soothing the digestive tract of an overfed feline!"

"I do not wish to contradict you, Doctor," Lt. Commander Data stated calmly, his synthetic arms holding the feline in question, "but I do not believe that I have fed Spot excessively." The gold-skinned android had arrived in sickbay only minutes before, bearing his afflicted pet. "Nevertheless, she has been gagging repeatedly for a period of 12.637 hours, which leads me to suspect the presence of a singularly stubborn *trichobezoar*."

"In other words, a hairball!" The EMH shook his balding head in disbelief. Ignoring the concerned android and his pet, he addressed Crusher petulantly. "Don't tell me you seriously intend to waste my considerable talents on a chore unworthy of even the most inexperienced orderly."

*Do you think I'd inflict your winning personality on a sentient patient?* the ship's chief medical officer asked silently. The fact that Reginald Barclay had played a significant part in the creation of the EMH didn't do anything to increase Beverly's confidence in the program.

"This is my sickbay," she reminded the hologram, asserting her authority, "and you'll treat whomever or whatever I assign you to." The tone of her voice made it clear that the discussion was over. "Mr. Data, hand over the patient."

With obvious care, the android passed the large orange tabby to the EMH, who grudgingly accepted his new charge. Spot, perhaps made cranky by her abdominal distress, was less than pleased by the transfer; hissing loudly, she snapped at the hologram's wrists with bared fangs, lashing out with her claws at the same time.

For a second it looked like the EMH was going to get bit, but the hologram evaded the tabby's jaws and paws by rendering the endangered portions of his anatomy momentarily intangible, so that the irate cat's attacks passed right through him. Holding Spot at arm's length, a disdainful expression on his face, the EMH carried the squirming feline over to the nearest biobed, then held the cat down on the sterile surface of the bed while its built-in diagnostic scanners examined Spot from the inside out. The whole time, the tabby struggled to escape the hologram's grip, alternating angry hisses with outraged yowls.

"You can keep your undoubtedly septic claws and teeth to yourself," the EMH sternly scolded his thrashing patient. "My program is more than a match for any presentient pussycat." He sighed and shook his head wearily. "Next they'll have me flossing the bicuspids of a Denebian slime devil!"

To distract Data from his pet's anxiety, and to better ignore the EMH's disaffected muttering, Beverly decided to initiate a little small talk. "So, how are our distinguished passengers faring?" she asked Data.

The *Enterprise* was currently transporting a shipload of alien ambassadors to a vital diplomatic conference on Penthara IV. Crusher suspected that Captain Picard had his hands full coping with the overinflated egos and fractious personalities of the quarreling delegates—a diagnosis that Data rapidly confirmed. "Our guests seem to be unusually . . . demanding," the android stated with admirable diplomacy. "They place an extraordinary amount of importance on their own preferences, to the exclusion of the concerns of their fellow ambassadors."

"I can imagine," Beverly said in a sympathetic tone. "Trying to get politicians to agree on anything, even the menu for a banquet, can be like herding cats."

On the biobed, a few meters away, Spot perked up her ears at

Crusher's remark, only to quickly lose interest in the conversation as it became apparent that Beverly wasn't going to use the C-word again anytime soon. She tried once more to bite the EMH, with more success this time. "Ouch!" the hologram yelped, his attention painfully yanked away from the diagnostic monitor above the bed. "That smarts!"

*Good thing holograms don't need tetanus shots,* Beverly thought, more amused than she probably ought to be by the EMH's stormy relationship with his patient. The sudden beep of her combadge, however, drove all thought of the EMH's predicament from her mind. "Crusher here," she said, tapping the gold duranium badge. "What is it?"

The voice of Captain Jean-Luc Picard came through the badge. "We have a medical emergency, Doctor. The Chelon ambassador has collapsed without warning. He is being beamed directly to sickbay."

"Understood," Crusher acknowledged. "We'll be ready."

*Or as ready as we can be,* she thought grimly. The Federation had only recently made contact with the Chelonae, so Beverly knew there was not a lot of information about this particular species in the Starfleet database. Nevertheless, she had made a point of familiarizing herself with the medical profiles of all the various alien species aboard (in fact, that's just what she'd been doing before Data showed up with Spot), so she was not at all surprised when a large humanoid turtle immediately materialized upon the primary biobed.

The golden sparkle of the transporter effect faded quickly, exposing a mottled, greenish-brown shell about the size of an adult Horta. Unfortunately, Crusher noted at once, the stricken Chelon had drawn his head and other extremities into his shell, leaving her little to examine except a dense, opaque carapace. *Thank goodness I don't need to rely on my eyes alone,* she thought, grateful for the state-of-the-art medical technology at her disposal.

"Alyssa!" she called out. Nurse Ogawa came running in from the adjacent medlab, where she had been performing tests on some experimental antibiotics. Since the unconscious ambassador would clearly not fit within the standard surgical support frame, Crusher was forced to rely on the overhead cluster of biofunction sensors; she also immediately activated a sterilization field around the biobed and its inaccessible occupant.

"Don't forget, I'm more than ready to assist you," the EMH volunteered, still contending with the uncooperative cat. Orange fur bristled all along Spot's back. "My program is fully equipped to deal with all manner of exoskeletons."

Beverly paid little attention to the hologram. She had more important things to concentrate on; the Chelon's vital signs were weak and fading steadily. She studied the diagnostic monitor, noting signs of severe cardiac distress. "Prepare for immediate surgery," she instructed Ogawa.

"Yes, Doctor," the nurse answered, hurrying to fetch a tray of gleaming exoscalpels, autosutures, and trilaser connectors. "You know," she commented upon her return, "in Japanese mythology, the turtle represents longevity and good luck."

"Let's hope that counts for something," Crusher said, frowning. They would have to work quickly to keep the ambassador alive.

The sickbay doors whished open, and Captain Picard marched briskly into the intensive-care ward, accompanied by another Chelon dignitary. The humanoid tortoise stood upright on his hind legs while his scaly, gray head poked out from the bony armor covering his torso. Aside from a copper medallion hanging from his squat, wattled neck, the Chelon wore no adornment; Beverly guessed that the terrapin's all-concealing shell made further garments unnecessary.

The captain hastily introduced the new arrival. "This is Secretary Skute, the ambassador's personal assistant."

"Is Ambassador Nanimult still alive?" the other Chelon croaked excitedly, pushing past Beverly to invade the sterilized area around his superior. "What are you doing to him?"

"Nothing yet," Crusher assured him. She tried to escort the agitated envoy away from the biobed, but Skute refused to budge. "But the ambassador's heart has undergone a serious rupture. He's hemorrhaging internally, which means I have to operate immediately to save his life."

"A rupture?" Skute's lower beak moved up and down rapidly. Glossy black eyes widened in surprise. "I don't understand. What could have caused this?"

"I'm not sure," Crusher told him. "That's going to take further investigation. First, though, we need to repair his heart as soon as possible."

"Make it so," Picard said. He placed his hand on the upper ridge of Skute's shell and politely but firmly indicated that the secretary should step back from the surgical area. "Ambassador Nanimult is in excellent hands," he promised the other Chelon.

But Skute appeared even more anxious than before. "Wait! Stop!" he squawked loudly, shrugging his shell out from beneath Picard's hand. Webbed hands gesticulated fussily. "You can't do this!"

Beverly didn't understand. Neither, judging from his puzzled expression, did the captain. "There's no choice," she explained. "I have to operate."

"No!" Skute insisted. "You don't understand. We are a very private people. It is strictly forbidden to allow one's shell to be opened in the presence of outsiders." Webbed fingers brushed his own shell protectively. "No offense intended, of course."

Beverly couldn't believe what she was hearing. "There's no way I can operate on the ambassador's heart without cutting through his shell somehow. We can't just stand by and let him die!"

"Ambassador Nanimult is a man of deep personal convictions," Skute stated flatly. "He would never violate our people's sacred customs and beliefs."

Picard attempted to reason with the Chelon envoy. "I respect your traditions, Secretary, but surely there must be some flexibility here. What is more important in this instance—propriety, or the ambassador's very survival?"

Skute shook his head vehemently. "With regret, Captain, I cannot possibly give your doctor permission to open Ambassador Nanimult's shell. You simply must save him without an invasive operation. Surely your Federation medical science has another solution?"

"But if this taboo is so important," Crusher protested, frustrated by the assistant's intransigence, "then why wasn't the ambassador traveling with a Chelon doctor, in case of emergency?" The nearest Chelon surgeon, she was all too aware, was hundreds of light-years away.

Skute sighed theatrically. "To be quite honest, Ambassador Nanimult was supposed to have been accompanied by his personal physician, but the doctor herself fell ill at the last minute, and there was no time to secure a replacement." His stubby tail twitched in a somewhat sheepish fashion. "The ambassador, who is a very . . . strong-willed . . . individual, has little patience with doctors at the best of times. He categorically refused to delay his departure until a new physician could be recruited, especially since he had just passed a routine check-up only a week before. That's just the way he is," Skute added apologetically.

Picard nodded soberly, prompting Beverly to guess that the captain could personally testify to the ambassador's "strong will" and stubbornness. "Jean-Luc," she beseeched him, "you have to let me save him."

"Blood pressure dropping to critical levels," Ogawa called out, adding urgency to Crusher's plea, as if any more were needed. They couldn't even set up a plasma I.V. without probing beneath Nanimult's shell.

Picard did not answer Crusher immediately. Scowling, he fixed a probing gaze on Secretary Skute, who stared back at the captain as adamantly and implacably as a Vulcan logician. Despite her overriding concern for her patient, Beverly couldn't help sympathizing with the captain's position; with so little known about the Chelonae and their beliefs, Picard had little choice but to accept Skute's pronouncements on Chelon culture.

Now it looked as though Nanimult's own obstinate nature, coupled with the Chelonae's strict sense of privacy, might cost the ambassador his life. Crusher had seldom felt so frustrated.

*I know I can save him,* she thought desperately, *if I can just get the chance!*

"Excuse me," the EMH interrupted, "but I may have a solution to this particular dilemma."

Beverly looked at the hologram in surprise. What with the crisis over the hemorrhaging ambassador, she had forgotten about the EMH and his veterinary duties. Her first impulse was to simply deactivate him—coping with that exasperating prima donna of a program was absolutely the last thing she needed right now—but she hesitated before voicing the necessary command. *It couldn't hurt to hear him out,* she realized; at this point, she was willing to listen to anyone who might know how to get around Secretary Skute's prohibitions.

Even an unusually obnoxious hologram.

"Well?" she prompted the EMH. "Go ahead."

The holographic doctor was momentarily taken aback by Crusher's invitation to speak, but he quickly recovered and launched into his proposed remedy. "By selectively turning my hands and instruments solid or intangible as needed, I should be able to operate on the ambassador's heart *through* the patient's shell, guided by the image on a medical monitor. That way, no primitive tribal taboos get violated; it's like the difference between a noninvasive scan for weapons and a strip search."

Picard's eyes lit up at the suggestion. "Yes," he said. "That could work." He eyed Skute confidently. "I can't imagine there are any centuries-old Chelon injunctions against X-rays and such; otherwise you would have already objected to our diagnostic sensors. Isn't that so, Secretary?"

Skute's wide black eyes zeroed in on the furry orange feline in the EMH's care, and his voice ascended to a new level of indignation: "I don't believe this. You seriously expect me to entrust Ambassador Nanimult's life to the ship's veterinarian?"

"I am not a veterinarian!" the EMH protested a bit too loudly, lifting Spot from the biobed and thrusting her gracelessly into Data's waiting arms. "I'll have you know, Mr. Secretary, that I am programmed with over five million possible treatments, two thousand medical references, forty-seven—"

"Our advanced Emergency Medical Hologram is completely reliable," Crusher asserted, cutting off the EMH's long-winded recitation of his attributes. *I can't believe I just said that,* she thought. "And he is a machine-generated phenomenon, just as X-rays are, so you should have no objection to using him to help the ambassador."

"I see, I mean, I don't know—" Skute waffled, his self-important manner proving no match against the combined resolve of the captain, Crusher, and the EMH. "I suppose it might be acceptable, but I'm not sure . . ."

Picard had heard all he needed to hear. "Get to work, Doctor," he instructed the EMH.

While the hologram raced against time to save Ambassador Nanimult, his intangible hands passing through the dense horn of the Chelon diplomat's shell, Beverly continued to study the sensor readings charting Nanimult's condition.

What she discovered disturbed her.

"Captain, if I may have a word with you in private?" She gestured toward her office at the opposite end of the ward. Her calm expression and level tone offered no clue as to what concerned her. "Data, why don't you join us?"

Leaving Nurse Ogawa to assist the EMH, she guided Picard and Data into her roomy office, then waited for the door to close automatically behind them before delivering the shocking news: "Captain, the ambassador has been poisoned."

*"Mon dieu,"* the captain whispered. "Are you quite certain, Doctor?"

Crusher nodded. "I checked the primary sensor readings against my medical tricorder and came to the same conclusion both times. Judging from the results, I'd guess that the toxin was administered, probably via a hypospray, sometime in the last six hours."

Picard's frown deepened. "Unfortunately, Ambassador Nanimult was attending a crowded reception in the ship's lounge when he was stricken; in the crush, any one of the ship's passengers could have poisoned him covertly. There are dozens of potential suspects."

"He could also have been poisoned in his own quarters, shortly before the reception," Crusher pointed out, "or en route to that same function."

Picard nodded. "In light of your discovery, Doctor, the sudden illness of the ambassador's physician, back on the Chelon home-world, now looks extremely suspicious, not to mention convenient. I suspect a conspiracy at work."

"Fascinating," Data observed, stroking Spot as he spoke. Beverly knew that the android enjoyed solving mysteries in the holodeck, often in the guise of Sherlock Holmes. "May I ask, Captain, if a hypospray was found at the site of the reception?"

"Not that I know of," Picard answered. "But I'll see to it that the lounge is immediately searched." He paused to consider what else might be done. "Inspecting the other ambassadors, their staffs, and their quarters will be a trickier proposition; the confidentiality of their persons and belongings is protected by diplomatic custom."

"Perhaps that will not be necessary," Data proposed. Cradled in the android's arms, Spot purred contentedly. "Chances are, the assassin will have wanted to dispose of the murder weapon as swiftly and efficiently as possible, and how better to do so than by dematerializing the hypospray in any one of the *Enterprise*'s many convenient replicator units?"

*That sounds logical enough,* Beverly thought.

The captain seemed intrigued. "Go on," he urged Data.

"What the assassin may not realize," Data stated, "is that the molecular patterns of all dematerialized refuse are held in the system's memory buffers for exactly 24.001 hours, on the off chance that someone accidentally disposes of something valuable, as has been occasionally known to happen."

"That's right," Beverly said. "I recovered my wedding ring that way once, after it slipped off my finger and got stuck in a surgical glove that I recycled before I knew what had happened." She vividly recalled her initial panic when she had first realized that the ring was missing. "Thank goodness the replicator was able to reproduce it perfectly."

Data approached Crusher's uncluttered desk. "May I use your terminal, Doctor?" Beverly stepped aside to let him pass, and Data seated himself before the doctor's primary workstation. Perhaps realizing that the android was going to be too busy to pet her anymore, Spot scooted off his lap and onto the floor, where she began nosing around the office. Data's fingers danced over the lighted control panel in a blur of superhuman speed. "I am instructing the computer to search its memory for anything resembling a hypospray that might have been disintegrated in a replicator in the last six hours."

Beverly held her breath expectantly, but the results of Data's search were not long in coming. An electronic chime announced that the ship's computer had completed its task. "My hypothesis was correct," Data reported promptly. "Computer records confirm that just such an operation occurred approximately 31.623 minutes before the start of the diplomatic reception."

"Commendable work, Mr. Data," Picard said. The captain leaned forward, determined to get to the bottom of the mystery. "Can the computer pinpoint the specific replicator unit used to destroy the weapon?"

"Affirmative, sir," Data revealed. "In fact, the replicator in question turns out to be located in the private quarters of "—Data raised an artificial eyebrow, presumably for dramatic effect— "Secretary Skute."

"Skute!" Crusher exclaimed. *No wonder that treacherous terrapin didn't want me to operate on Ambassador Nanimult . . . !*

"Indeed," Data continued, rising from the doctor's chair. "I theorize that Skute poisoned the ambassador shortly before the reception, then covertly disposed of the incriminating hypospray in his own quarters, which happen to be adjacent to those of Ambassador Nanimult."

The captain tapped his combadge. "Picard here. Security to sickbay, on the double." A stern, unforgiving expression came over his dignified features. "Now then, let's go see to the ambassador's oh-so-solicitous subordinate."

Beverly and Data followed Picard back to the intensive-care ward, where they found Skute fidgeting at the fringes of the surgical area. Two imposing assistant nurses, no doubt drafted by Ogawa, flanked the secretary, keeping him more or less out of the way of the EMH and Nurse Ogawa as they labored to repair the damage to the ambassador's heart. Crusher glanced quickly at the monitor above the biobed and was relieved to see that Nanimult's life signs were weak but stable. An infusion of an all-purpose plasma substitute was helping to raise the patient's blood pressure. *I think I may have underestimated the EMH's talents,* she admitted privately, *even if his personality still leaves something to be desired.*

"Please step away from the ambassador, Secretary," Picard ordered in his most authoritative tone, even as a steel door slid open to admit a team of security officers in red-and-black uniforms, each one with a hand on the phaser at his or her hip.

Skute blinked in alarm. Beverly could tell that the would-be assassin knew his guilt had been exposed. His left arm retracted into his shell, and Crusher half expected the rest of his extremities to follow; instead, the skittish forelimb suddenly reemerged, gripping a lethal-looking disruptor pistol, which Beverly assumed came from some form of inner pouch. "Stay back!" Skute squawked, brandishing his weapon wildly. "I'll kill you all if I have to!"

His holographic hands still deeply immersed in the unconscious ambassador, the EMH looked up in annoyance. "If you don't mind," he objected, sounding distinctly vexed by the confrontation brewing in sickbay, "I'm performing a very complicated surgical procedure here, so I'd appreciate a little less commotion."

Although somewhat lacking in perspective, the EMH had a point, Beverly realized; an intensive-care ward was no place for a shoot-out. Captain Picard understood that, too. "Everyone keep back," he instructed all present, gesturing for the assistant nurses to distance themselves from the desperate Skute. "Listen to me, Secretary. Don't get yourself into any deeper trouble than you're already in. If you put down that weapon, I'll see to it that you get a fair trial on your homeworld."

"No!" Skute blurted, his lower beak quivering. The prospect of answering for his crime clearly horrified him. "I want a shuttle," he insisted, "and two days' head start!" Cold black eyes darted from left to right and back again, perhaps trying to pick out the most suitable hostage. A chill ran down Beverly's spine as Skute's gaze settled on her. "You," he decided, nodding at Crusher. "Get over here."

"Belay that order, Doctor," Picard said firmly. Holding his hands palms up to demonstrate that he wasn't armed, the captain stepped between Skute and Crusher. He spoke slowly and evenly, so as not to panic the gun-wielding Chelon. "Your scheme has failed, Skute. You might as well surrender, and tell us who put you up to this." He took a single, cautious step toward Skute.

"Stop! I'm warning you!" Skute aimed his disruptor directly at Picard, while keeping one eye on the rest of the room's occupants. The only individual the assassin wasn't watching out for was Spot, padding silently behind him on four stealthy paws. In re-

40

sponse to Picard's advance toward him, the terrapin stepped backward and tripped over the underfoot feline. His rigid shell crashed hard against the floor.

Taking prompt advantage, Picard dashed forward and kicked the disruptor out of the startled Chelon's grip. The weapon spun away from Skute's webbed fingers while the disarmed assassin rocked helplessly on the floor, unable (like any other tortoise) to right himself without assistance.

"Good cat, Spot!" Data raised his pet, who merely rubbed herself against Picard's leg.

"So, it seems," Picard explained to the recovering ambassador, "that Skute was secretly affiliated with a group of fanatical isolationists and xenophobes. He'd hoped that your suspicious death, in the presence of so many non-Chelonae, would turn your people against the prospect of closer relations with the Federation."

"Well, even if that's what Skute intended, I'm afraid he's achieved rather the opposite effect." Ambassador Nanimult was recuperating in sickbay, his bed propped up at an angle to allow him to recline comfortably within his shell. His wrinkled head resembled Skute's, beak and all, but there was a silvery tint to his scales, and his dry, gray flesh, visible at last, was even more wizened. "This unfortunate incident has only raised my opinion of the Federation and its representatives. I am deeply indebted to you and your doctors, Captain."

"I'm glad we were able to help you in time," Beverly said, "despite the best efforts of Secretary Skute."

"Former Secretary," Nanimult said, correcting her. He shook his head slowly, visibly troubled by his erstwhile assistant's duplicity. "What he told you was partly correct, Doctor. We are a deeply private people, some of us more private than others. But no sensible Chelon would ever shun life-saving surgery simply to protect the sanctity of his or her shell. Only a fanatic like Skute could have presented such a ludicrous argument with a straight face."

"Clearly, Skute had his own reasons for trying to prevent Dr. Crusher from operating on you," Picard observed. The scheming secretary had been confined to the brig until such time as he could be safely handed over to the Chelon authorities. "Although we could not have known that at the time."

*Thankfully, we found a way around Skute's stringent prohibitions,* Beverly thought, which reminded her of something else she needed to take care of. One final courtesy. "Activate Emergency Medical Hologram."

Like a genie summoned from a lamp, the EMH materialized at the foot of the bed, between Crusher and Picard. "Please state the nature of the medical emergency," he requested, per the inflexible dictates of his programming.

"No emergency," Crusher informed him, then turned back toward Nanimult. "Ambassador, I'd like you to meet the surgeon who actually performed the operation that saved your life."

Although startled by the hologram's abrupt appearance, Nanimult, veteran diplomat that he was, recovered his aplomb with admirable speed. "You have my gratitude, sir," he croaked heartily.

Beverly smiled. "I'd like to thank you as well, Doctor," she said, realizing, with a touch of contrition, that she had never before addressed the EMH that way. "Your assistance was invaluable."

For once, the usually argumentative hologram was speechless. A look of open gratitude appeared upon his photonically generated face, and he gulped nervously, seemingly overcome with emotion, before replying. "You're welcome, Doctor. You don't know how much that means to me." His posture stiffened as he regained his composure. "And may I add that I admired the persuasive manner with which you convinced that irritating turtle-person to let me operate."

"Thanks." *That wasn't so hard,* Beverly thought, enjoying the first cordial conversation she had ever had with the prickly holographic physician. *Maybe I need to work on thinking of the EMH as a potential colleague, rather than a bothersome piece of soft-ware.* She savored the ambassador's salutary return from near death. *Who knows? This could be the beginning of a fruitful working relationship.*

*Of course, he's still going to have to work on that abominable bedside manner of his. . . .*

## SHIP'S MEDICAL LOG, STARDATE 52501.6

*Ambassador Nanimult is responding well to treatment and, provided he doesn't overexert himself, should be able to take part in the conference by the time we reach Penthara IV. All relevant medical records have already been transmitted via subspace to the medical staff at the conference.*

*And, oh yes, after an application of liquid paraffin, taken internally, Spot successfully disgorged a rather revolting clump of matted fur. Regular doses of replicated pumpkin mash have been prescribed to prevent any further recurrence of her symptoms.*

# On the Scent of Trouble

## By John Gregory Betancourt

*Captain's Log, Supplemental*
*As the* Enterprise *nears the Pelavos star cluster, long-range sensors are detecting signs of an advanced civilization—six planets and ten moons have been terraformed and colonized. Clearly the beings who live here are spacefaring and highly intelligent. Starfleet has directed us to postpone our star-charting assignment in order to make contact with the Pelavians.*

"Sir," said Commander Data, turning in his seat at the navigator's console. His yellow eyes widened slightly, but Captain Jean-Luc Picard knew it was from programming rather than worry or excitement. "I am picking up a ship on impulse power."

"On screen," Picard said, leaning forward. He felt a familiar rush of excitement at the thought of first contact. No matter how old he became, no matter how many times he did it, encountering an alien species for the first time always excited him. He glanced at his second-in-command, Commander William Riker, who sat to his right. Riker hid it well, but Picard had known him long enough to read below that exterior calm: *He feels the thrill, too.*

"Will it be *their* first contact?" Riker mused. He scratched his chin through his beard thoughtfully.

"Let's hope so, Number One. We're close enough to the Romulan Neutral Zone that they could have beaten us here decades ago."

"Don't forget the Ferengi," ship's counselor Deanna Troi said from the seat to Picard's left. "They have been active in this area, too."

"Also true." He nodded. The Ferengi had been exploring the galaxy long before the United Federation of Planets came into existence. On several occasions Starfleet ships had encountered new races only to discover the Ferengi had been there first—pillaging in the name of profit. "Let's hope it goes well."

An image appeared on the viewscreen at the front of the bridge, showing a spherical silver ship with no sign of viewports or openings of any kind. In space, it was often hard to guess the size of an object; you didn't have enough reference points against the greater cosmic vastness. Yet something told Picard—some instinct, some premonition—that this was a small ship, at least as compared to the *Enterprise.*

As though reading his mind, Data said, "The Pelavian vessel is approximately thirty-two meters in diameter. Scanners detect twenty-two life forms on board."

"Distance?" Picard asked.

"Fifteen thousand four hundred ten kilometers," Data said. "And closing."

"Full stop."

"Aye, sir."

Picard leaned forward, studying the ship. What kind of people would leave out viewports? Didn't they want to see the stars?

"Hail them," he said.

A second later, Worf replied, "There is no response, sir."

"What is their weapons status?"

"None that I can detect, sir."

"Are they scanning us?"

Data said, "Apparently not, sir. I am picking up no transmissions of any kind."

"Curious." Picard leaned back on one elbow, considering the situation. No scans, no viewports, no weapons. Clearly this was a most unusual species.

"Their ship contains an oxygen-nitrogen atmosphere that should be compatible with our own," Data went on. "Their artificial gravity reads at one-point-oh-six Earth normal."

Beside Picard, Deanna suddenly sat rigidly upright. "I am sensing something!" she said.

"What is it?" Picard asked. Her empathic abilities had saved the *Enterprise* on more than one occasion.

"They are telepaths . . . very powerful . . . trying to contact us—"

"Can you talk to them?"

"I am not a telepath, Captain . . . it's like I am overhearing their thoughts."

He nodded slightly. "What are they saying?"

"I sense confusion from the Pelavians—perhaps because we have not responded to their hails." She paused. "It's hard to understand—wait! I think they sense me!"

Picard said, "Are they reading your thoughts? Can you let them know them we mean them no harm?"

"I am not sure. They do not seem hostile, just confused."

"If possible, ask them to meet with us."

A sudden mew of pain came from Deanna, and her face drained of blood. Her eyes rolled back as she slumped a little in her seat.

"Can't—" she gasped.

"Deanna!" Riker said, leaping to his feet.

Picard raised one hand, restraining him. "Are you all right, Counselor?" he demanded. "Were you telepathically attacked?"

"No." She shook her head almost groggily. "I'm sorry, sir. The Pelavians are . . . *different* from other telepaths I have encountered. They use sense-impressions as much as words. Trying to understand it all was too much for me."

"Did you learn anything?" Riker asked.

"They accepted our invitation," she said.

Picard blinked. "Our invitation—"

"To meet with them."

"Sir," said Data. "I believe you should see this."

Picard glanced at the viewscreen. The bottom of the spherical ship had begun to peel back in sections, almost like a flower opening to morning light. A smaller round ship darted out, then began to accelerate toward the *Enterprise.*

"The Pelavian ambassadors are on their way," Deanna said softly. "Their names . . ." She hesitated. "I—don't know how to translate," she said. "Their names are telepathic impressions, somewhere between the scent of chocolate and the texture of cream—that's as close as I can come. It does not translate."

"There are two life forms on board," Data said.

"Prepare Shuttle Bay Two," Picard said. "They can land there. Deanna? Can you convey that?"

"I believe so." She shut her eyes, then a moment later nodded. Picard noticed that she had begun to grow pale again, and her hands shook slightly. Clearly she could not stand prolonged contact with the Pelavians. They would have to use her talent sparingly.

"Deanna?" he asked softly.

"Yes," she whispered. "They understand."

Suddenly her eyes fluttered and she slumped again. She would have fallen to the deck if he hadn't caught her.

With Riker's help, Picard lifted her back into her seat. Then he tapped his combadge.

"Picard to sickbay. Send a medical team to the bridge."

Doctor Crusher's voice replied: "On our way. What's the problem?"

"Counselor Troi appears to have fainted."

"I'm all right now . . ." Deanna said, struggling to pull herself up. "I do not need medical attention."

"Are you certain?" he asked.

"Yes." She sat straighter, massaging her temples. "I just have a headache. I'll be fine. I was overwhelmed by their, ah, *enthusiasm.*"

He leaned back. "Very well. Belay that order, Doctor."

"Yes, Jean-Luc—but I still want to look her over."

Deanna said, "As soon as the Pelavian ambassadors are safely aboard, I promise to stop by, Beverly."

"I'll hold you to that. Crusher out."

Riker said, "You mentioned being overwhelmed by their enthusiasm—what does *that* mean?"

Deanna hesitated. "They think too quickly, too loud, too . . ." She shrugged helplessly. "I cannot put into words quite what they did. It's kind of like overthinking someone—you would have to be a telepath to truly understand. My mother did it to me a couple of times by accident when I was a child, only the Pelavians are a hundred times more powerful than she is."

"It's almost enough to make me wish your mother were here," Picard said wryly.

Riker gave a wicked grin. "It *can* be arranged, sir—"

"No, no!" He raised his hands in surrender. "No need to go overboard, Number One. Enthusiastic Pelavians are quite enough for one day." He turned to Data. "How long until they reach us?"

"Approximately twenty-six minutes at their present speed, sir."

He nodded, rising. Just enough time to get cleaned up and put on his dress uniform. "Very well. You have the bridge, Mr. Worf.

Counselor, Mr. Data, Number One—you will join the greeting party. You have twenty minutes to change."

As planned, Captain Picard met Riker, Data, and Deanna Troi in Shuttle Bay Two at the appointed time. Pulling his long red dress tunic a little straighter, Picard gave an approving nod to each of his senior staff. All looked more than presentable for such an important meeting.

He turned as the shuttle bay's huge double doors began to open, revealing velvety black dotted with stars. A silver sphere glided out of the darkness. As it passed between the shuttle bay's doors, the force field sheltering them from the vacuum of space flickered faintly.

Then the little ship slowly settled onto the flight deck, extending three stabilizing feet for balance. The low hum of its engines faded. A heartbeat later, a front panel dilated open, and Picard found himself gazing into an unlighted chamber. He could just make out some kind of safety webbing, smooth machinery with visible finger-controls, and plenty of handholds.

*No viewports,* he thought, as realization settled in. *No lights. They must be blind.*

"Deanna?" he asked.

"I sense an intense curiosity," she said. "They mean us no harm. That much is clear."

Just as he had expected. "Good."

Slowly two aliens stepped out of their shuttle. Both were short and thickly built, with stubby legs that ended in rounded white pads almost like an elephant's. Their three-fingered hands were small and delicate. A fine white fur covered their elongated torsos. They had small, perfectly round heads—but without eyes, ears, or nose. Tiny puckered mouths stood out from their faces on small fleshy stalks. Other than that, they had no sensory organs of any kind that he could see. Then he spotted a slight flutter of movement on their chests beneath the white fur. He tried not to stare at a line of tiny slitted gill-like openings almost hidden there.

But he could smell them: Soft, almost musky scents tickled his nose, something like fresh corn mingled with vanilla and caraway, then sulfur and coffee and something sweeter than honey. It made his head swim.

"They are making sounds far above the range of human hearing," Data whispered. "But I am unable to discern any linguistic pattern. May I proceed with my scan?"

"Surreptitiously, Mr. Data."

"Of course, sir."

Ten seconds had passed with no action on either side. It was time to get things moving. And, as host, clearly it was up to Picard to take the initiative.

He stepped forward. "I am captain Jean-Luc Picard of the United Federation of Planets," he said firmly. "I wish to welcome you aboard the *Enterprise.*"

Both Pelavians hopped back away from him. Their arms flapped frantically. He heard a faint, high-pitched squeal.

"Too loud," Deanna whispered. "I feel their shock and pain and disorientation."

Data surreptitiously raised a medical tricorder and began a scan of their bodies. "They are like no other race we have encountered before," he said softly. "I cannot identify the functions of many of their internal organs. But they have what appears to be a highly developed echolocation system."

"Like bats?" Riker said.

"Exactly. They send out sound waves to map the area around them. They have no eyes as we understand them."

:YOU ARE PRIME?:

The words suddenly filled Picard's head, driving out all other thoughts. *Sulfur, the texture of clay, a taste like copper on the back of the tongue.* He opened his mouth. Light flashed behind his eyes. He felt drunk and disoriented, as if he stood in many places at once and saw himself as a warm shape through his *thbok*-senses.

Thbok-*senses?*

And abruptly the presence waned like a receding tide. It left him confused and gasping like a fish out of water.

He realized his officers were staring at him curiously.

"Sir?" Riker asked. "Are you all right?"

"They touched your mind," Deanna said. "I felt it, too."

"Yes," he said softly. He blinked and tried to put his words in order. Slowly he looked at the Pelavians. Something still tickled at the back of his head, and he suspected they were reading his surface thoughts.

*Yes, I am the commander here.* He thought the words clearly, wondering if they could pick them up. *No wonder Deanna became overwhelmed.* He hadn't been able to hold a coherent thought while they were in his head.

:We Greet You, Prime.:

This time the words came more softly, as though they understood the problem and held back in their contact. The words mingled with tastes and smells and sense-impressions, so many and so fast that he could not quite follow them. Their thought-language was as rich with texture as any he had ever encountered, and he rapidly realized that he must be grasping only a tiny part of their mental dialogue.

"Welcome aboard the *Enterprise*," he said, thinking the words as precisely as he spoke them. "We are pleased whenever we encounter a new people."

He caught a scent of fresh-mown hay, and the sense came to him that the Pelavians, too, were pleased. They seemed to almost glow with happiness.

:We are not alone in the universe.:

"No," he said quickly. Apparently this was a true first contact. "Many different people live throughout our galaxy."

:Tell us more your worlds.:

\* \* \*

To Picard's satisfaction, things moved smoothly after that. After relating as much of the history of the United Federation of Planets as seemed appropriate, he led the Pelavians on a tour of his ship, beginning with the shuttle bays. They touched his mind briefly whenever they had questions, and he answered them verbally, knowing they could read his thoughts. This system of communication seemed to work quite well.

As the tour progressed, he made certain he stood close to them, breathing in the sweet scents they seemed to exude so readily. Vanilla mingled with wild berries, Arcturian honeycombs tinged with lilac and rosemary—so many different scents.

When they entered engineering, the two Pelavians stood before the warp core. They remained silent, examining it with senses that Picard could not begin to guess at.

His other officers gathered around for a quick conference, and Geordi La Forge hurried over to join them.

"Is there anything I can do to help with your guests?" the chief engineer asked a little hesitantly. "They seem a little, well, hard to reach."

"Let me handle them," Picard said. This was his tour, and he had no intention of letting his crew steal the glory. The Pelavians were *his*.

"My assessment of their physiology is done, sir," Data said. "They are communicating with each other not only telepathically, but through sensory emitters in their gills, which release streams of complex airborne chemicals."

"Airborne chemicals?" Riker said, frowning.

"Those smells—" Deanna said.

Data looked at her blankly. "Smells?"

"Yes," Picard said. It all clicked together. He knew exactly what Deanna meant. "Whenever they touched my mind, I smelled something. Usually something sweet."

Data said, "The chemicals do not remain in the air, but break down fairly quickly. I beleive they are designed to enhance tele-pathic communications—a chemical 'body language,' if you will."

"Interesting," Riker said. "I don't think I have ever heard of a species that uses scent for communication."

"Most species, including humans, use scent to enhance com-munications," Data said. "Consider your own pheromones, sir. They tell women when you are sexually attracted to them."

"Er . . . yes," Riker said. Picard thought he was a little embar-rassed by the comment. "Pheromones, right."

Picard glanced at the Pelavians. *I need to get back to them. And I need to get rid of the others.*

To Riker, he said, "I'll finish from here, Number One. You may return to your duties."

"Very good, sir," Riker said, a trifle too slowly for Picard's lik-ing. "I'll be on the bridge if you need me."

*I'll make sure I don't, Number One,* Picard thought. He no longer wanted Riker around, but he couldn't quite say why. *He's always been insolent. Always been after my ship and my com-mand.*

"And I should see Doctor Crusher," Deanna Troi said. "I promised her I would stop in. I still don't feel completely well."

Picard nodded. "Do so. Take your time. I can handle the Pela-vians myself." That would be best. He could keep them for him-self and not have to worry about the others stabbing him in the back.

"Very well, sir."

"Shall I continue to accompany you?" Data asked. "My duty shift is up now, but I would appreciate the opportunity to study them."

Picard narrowed his eyes. Data was another one he had to watch, he thought. All that android precision . . . it would be easy for Data to steal his command.

"No," he said. "Why don't you begin an analysis of the Pelavians' scent-communication? Perhaps you can adapt the universal translator to use it."

"An intriguing idea, sir. If I could enlist Geordi's assistance?"

"By all means," Picard said. That would keep them both busy. Too busy to interfere with him.

He rejoined the Pelavians. "Shall we continue our tour?" he asked.

On the way to the turbolift, Commander Riker sagged against the wall. His eyes ached. His head ached. He felt sick and nervous and jittery all at once.

Then the walls began to melt around him, flowing like molten plastic, down, down, down. He gaped. He blinked.

And just as suddenly it was gone. Two ensigns had paused to stare at him.

"Are you all right, sir?" one asked.

"Yes," he snapped back. "You're not getting my job that way, Ensign Parker!"

Straightening, he ran down the hall for the turbolift. *They won't stop me,* he thought. *Nobody can stop me.*

"Sickbay," Deanna Troi told the turbolift.

It whisked her toward the proper deck. But when the doors opened, she stepped out into a garden. Flowers grew everywhere. She stared, as they began to move, vines writhing and tangling, stalks twisting, flowers opening like mouths and snapping at her—

And just as suddenly they were gone. She leaned against the wall for a second, pressing her eyes closed. *I really have been working too hard,* she thought. Stress and the Pelavians—that had to be the answer. Just to make sure, she'd tell Beverly about it. She didn't think there would be a medical cause, but it wouldn't hurt to find out.

Shaking her head, she hurried toward sickbay.

\* \* \*

"These are the plasma ducts," Captain Picard said. "They channel raw plasma to the reactor core."

He sensed slight puzzlement from his guests, but did not elaborate on the matter/antimatter fusion process. Some things had to be kept secret, after all.

All around him, La Forge's engineers were staring. They looked back at their work as soon as he turned his head, but he could *feel* them staring. Data and La Forge busied themselves at one of the workstations, and they seemed intent on equipping a portable universal translator with some kind of sensor panel.

The walls wavered.

*I'm hallucinating,* he thought. But now the Pelavians were looking at him again, and he knew he would have to keep them moving, keep them distracted, or they might begin to suspect. After all, who could he trust to take over the tour? Not Riker—not Data or Worf or Deanna Troi. *Nobody.* He was alone in his command. Riker was after the *Enterprise.* Picard narrowed his eyes. He had never trusted Riker. In fact, his whole senior staff was out to get him. He'd have to carry on by himself. He was the only one he could trust.

:We are done here, Prime?:

"Yes . . . *yes,*" he said. The scent of charcoal and apple cider surrounded him. "We will see the ship's astrogation labs next."

He hesitated, glancing sidelong at Data and La Forge, who were still pretending to ignore him. He knew they were eavesdropping on every word he said, though. *They want me dead. I need protection.*

Protection—why hadn't he thought of it before? He smiled grimly to himself, then tapped his combadge.

"Picard to Worf. Have a security team meet me in engineering on the double."

"Aye, sir," Worf said. "Is something wrong?"

"No!"

Worf—he was another one. Always scowling, angry, afraid. *I'll have to watch him, too.*

55

"Picard out!" he said.

:Are you well?: the Pelavians asked in his mind.

"Yes!" he snapped, mentally and verbally. He glanced around. Everyone was staring at him now, and they made no pretense of hiding it.

"Sir!" said a man's voice from behind him. "Ensigns Ordover and DeCandido reporting for duty!"

Picard jumped a bit, then whirled. Two men stood there stiffly, awaiting his orders.

"Fall in behind our guests," he said. "Watch for assassins."

"Assassins?" Ordover said. "Sir—do you think—"

"Just follow orders, Ensign."

Turning, he stalked toward the door. The Pelavians followed, bringing the scent of cedar chips and cinnamon.

Dr. Beverly Crusher brushed back her hair with one hand as she raised the medical scanner over Deanna Troi's forehead. It whirred faintly.

"I don't see anything that could cause hallucinations," she said, frowning a bit. "I'm showing slightly elevated adrenaline levels, but that's not very unusual."

Deanna sat up, smoothing her dress. "So what caused the hallucination?"

Dr. Crusher sighed. "You fainted on the bridge. Perhaps telepathic contact with the Pelavians had something to do with it. I don't know what else it could be at this point. Let me know if it happens again."

The walls tilted. Captain Picard felt as though he were walking up the side of a mountain, into a stiff wind, surrounded by the scents of pine and boiling cabbage. *Not much farther,* he told himself, touching the wall to keep his balance. *Only a few steps more.*

A door slid open and Deanna Troi lunged out at him. Picard drew up short, staring. *She's up to something.*

56

"Captain," she said, "are you all right? You don't look well. You're sweating—"

"I—am—fine!" He straightened and tried to ignore the way the deck moved underfoot.

"I sense some emotional turbulence," Deanna said. "I think you should see Doctor Crusher for a checkup. You're at the sickbay, after all—"

"Sickbay!" He took a step back. *What am I doing here? I was heading for astrogation!*

"Sir—"

"I don't need your interference, Counselor! I am perfectly capable of running this ship without your meddling!"

"Sir—I would never interfere in the way you run this ship."

"I know what you're up to! You're trying to subvert my authority so Riker can take over! I know how you feel about him—don't deny it!"

She sighed. "Sir, I once had intimate feelings for Will, but that was a long time ago."

Yes, he saw the whole plot now. "You're relieved of duty. Consider yourself confined to quarters."

"Captain—"

He didn't hear her next words. To his horror, her face began to twitch. Her cheeks bulged, and suddenly black metal sprouted . . . Borg implants. Her skin scaled over. Her eyes went dead and black. A device on her right arm whirred.

"We are the Borg," she told him in a cold voice. "Resistance is futile. Put down your weapons and prepare to be assimilated."

"Shoot her!" Picard cried, backpedaling furiously. The Pelavians caught him, squeaking like bats, wrapping him in smells of panic-filled burnt rubber. "Shoot her! She's a Borg!"

The two ensigns leaped forward, phasers drawn, but they did not fire. The room tilted. They stared past the Borg as if they couldn't see it.

"Shoot!" he screamed. "That's an order!"

The Borg that had been Deanna Troi took a step forward. It raised its hand. Picard saw the targeting device attached to it and knew she meant to take him down.

"Fall back!" he shouted. He seized the Pelavians by their arms and hustled them away, up the bucking corridor floor, up a sudden and endless hill. They could take cover in hydroponics, he thought. He could organize the resistance from cover.

As Deanna Troi rode the turbolift to the bridge, she found herself trembling. She had never seen the captain act so . . . crazed.

A red alert began to sound. Overhead, the red warning light flashed and the klaxon began to blare its familiar *whoop-whoop-whoop*. Then the turbolift's doors whisked open and she stepped out into a scene of panic and chaos.

Worf, at his security station, barked commands to security teams. Data stood at the internal sensors, his hands moving so quickly that they blurred. Only Riker sat perfectly still in the captain's seat, the eye of the storm, watching everyone grimly and listening to their reports.

"Security teams report Decks Eight through Twelve free of Borg infiltration!" Worf called.

"What's going on?" Deanna demanded, joining Riker. "What Borg? The captain started screaming about them outside of sickbay, pointing at me and telling his security escort to shoot. For an instant, I thought they were going to do it, too!"

"The captain did *what?*" He stared at her incredulously.

She nodded. "He seemed to think I was Borg. I sensed a great disturbance in him, but he refused to go to sickbay."

Riker frowned, stroking his beard. "That may help explain what's going on—the captain has been reporting Borg presence on four different decks, but internal sensors and security sweeps haven't found any sign of them. Normally I'd think this was some kind of security test, but with the Pelavian ambassadors aboard . . ."

58

She nodded. "It doesn't make sense."

The intercom suddenly crackled and the captain's voice boomed: "Get to work changing the phaser modulation! The Borg are on Deck Six! I need more men now!"

"On their way, sir!" Worf said. He quickly dispatched six more men to Deck Six.

Riker sat back. "Clearly it's not a real Borg invasion," he said. "Could it be a telepathic attack? Do you think the Pelavians are testing us, somehow?"

"I don't think so," Deanna said. "The Pelavians are entirely peaceful. They have never contacted any other race . . . let alone the Borg."

"Nevertheless, I think we would be best served if we got them off the ship. For their own safety, if nothing else."

She nodded. "I think you're right."

"I will take care of it, sir," Data said. He changed to the transporter station, adjusted the controls, and announced, "I have locked onto them. I am beaming them directly to their own ship."

"The Borg have captured the Pelavians!" Picard shouted. "What's going on up there? Report!"

Riker tapped his combadge. "Riker to Captain Picard. We have beamed the Pelavians back to their ship for their own safety. Please stand by. We are continuing sensor sweeps to locate the Borg."

The captain did not reply.

Riker looked at Troi. "So what's wrong with him, Deanna? I need answers!"

"Perhaps the captain is hallucinating." Deanna hesitated, remembering the way he had looked at her outside the turbolift. *He didn't see me. He looked right through me.* "Earlier today, after I left the captain in engineering, I suffered a mild hallucination myself. I headed for sickbay, but I found myself in a corridor filled with flowers. It seemed completely real for a second . . . but then it was gone. Doctor Crusher seemed to think it was due to stress. But now I wonder . . ."

Riker blanched. "I had a similar episode when I left engineering," he said.

"What happened? More flowers?"

"The walls started to melt. But it only lasted a second. I put it down to stress—"

She nodded. "Perhaps it's related to the overthinking. The Pelavians were in mental contact with Captain Picard and me."

"But not me," Riker said pointedly.

"It might have spilled over to you."

He hesitated. "But it only lasted a second. The captain—"

"Has been around them constantly. And it seems his hallucinations have not only continued, but grown worse."

Riker turned to Data. "Where is the captain now?"

"In hydroponics, sir."

Worf said, "Phasers are being fired there!"

"Is the captain alone?"

"He is accompanied by eighteen security guards."

Riker bit his lip. "Flood the room with anesthezine gas," he said.

"Sir?" Data said.

"You heard me. Do it!"

Data shrugged a little, but did as instructed. Deanna knew what would be happening: the colorless, odorless gas would be flooding into the room, rendering everyone unconscious within a few seconds.

Riker rose. "You have the bridge, Mr. Data," he said. He tapped his combadge. "Riker to Doctor Crusher. Please meet me in hydroponics. Bring your medical teams."

Hydroponics was a disaster. As Riker stepped through the doorway, he found himself splashing through pools of spilled nutrients. Tables had been overturned, and phaser burns scarred the walls.

Security officers sprawled everywhere. After a second, he spotted Captain Picard in the corner, behind an overturned planter of Vulcan creepers.

"Captain," he said, bending. A second later, Dr. Crusher joined him. She administered a shot to the captain's neck, and a second later his eyes fluttered open.

"Number One . . ." he said groggily. "Where am I?"

"In hydroponics, sir." He swallowed. "There was a firefight, so I flooded the room with anesthezine gas."

Slowly Picard levered himself up to a sitting position. Riker took one arm and Dr. Crusher the other, and together they got him to his feet. He winced and touched his head.

"I feel terrible." Then he seemed to remember. "The Borg—"

"Never here." Riker shook his head. "You appeared to be hallucinating. Deanna and I had episodes, too, but ours were brief. We can only guess the Pelavians had something to do with it."

"You beamed them back to their ship?"

"That's right."

Deanna Troi joined them. "I just spoke with them again," she said. "They are quite confused. I assured them that what happened was unusual—to say the least!—and I think they understood."

"Good work, all of you," Picard said. He swayed a little, and Riker steadied his arm. "Now, let's see if we can get to the bottom of this!"

*Captain's Log, supplemental*
*Dr. Crusher's tests proved conclusively that the chemicals that the Pelavians exhale cause hallucinations in humans. They break down fairly quickly in open air, but when they are inhaled, they enter the bloodstream. Prolonged exposure leads to hallucinations and paranoid delusions. Fortunately, Dr. Crusher has already begun work on a solution. . . .*

As the shimmering beams of light dissipated, Captain Picard stepped forward to greet the two Pelavian ambassadors standing on the transporter cells. He smiled and extended his arms in greeting. After a second's hesitation, they did the same.

:We greet you, Prime.: they thought to him.

"I welcome you once more to the *Enterprise*," he said. His voice sounded a little stuffy, he thought, due to the special nose filters Dr. Crusher had designed to remove the airborne chemicals. "I assure you, this time our meeting will not be interrupted."

:You are well now?:

"Yes, thank you. Shall we continue our tour?"

Turning, he started for sickbay. "Our chief medical officer was able to discover the cause of our problems through computer simulations . . ." he began. As the Pelavians read his thoughts, he thought he sensed a deep fascination in them.

Yes, this seemed like a good start to the relationship between their peoples. *A successful first contact. I like the smell of this,* he thought with a smile.

# Life Itself Is Reason Enough

## By M. Shayne Bell

*CAPTAIN'S LOG: STARDATE 47736.1.*

*We are continuing to assist in the evacuation of several colony worlds in Sector 225 that have entered deadly ionized dust clouds. This strange phenomenon is so thick that it blocks all planets from necessary light and heat. At the current rate, the atmospheric gases will soon freeze, cascade down to the planets, and extinguish all life.*

*We are leading one hundred eighty-three merchant ships, scientific vessels, even the odd sailing yacht to Nunanavik, an arctic world settled by Inuit from Earth. The dust makes transporter use impossible, so we are forced to rely on shuttles—but the* Enterprise *and the ships with us do not have enough vehicles to carry away all of Nunanavik's people. Other ships are rushing to help, but it appears they will not arrive in time.*

*The nearest starship is the* Carpathia. *At this rate, it will reach Nunanavik two hours after atmosphere collapse. Unlike its namesake, which at least managed to pick up survivors from the old aquatic vessel* Titanic, *this* Carpathia *will find no one left to save.*

Lieutenant Worf unbolted the last of the shelves in the personnel shuttle *Hawking* and passed it out the door. Removing the shelving made room for at least four more people. The Klingon officer wiped the sweat off his forehead and began gathering his tools.

"Worf?"

It was Deanna Troi. Worf turned and smiled despite himself. Ever since he and Deanna had shared dinner and champagne on his birthday, it had been harder not to smile when she was near.

"I found these straps in storage," she said. "I was thinking that we could bolt them to the walls and give people something to hang onto during flight."

"An excellent idea," Worf said. He took one of the straps from her hands and looked at it. "We can screw them into the holes where the shelving was bolted to the walls."

"I'll hunt up some screws and washers," Deanna said.

Worf nodded. "We'll need to punch holes in the tops of these straps. I'll get a tool to do that."

They both started down the ramp.

"Aren't you supposed to be sleeping?" Worf asked.

"Yes, and you are, too."

They set off in opposite directions. Worf looked back at Deanna more than once.

Eventually, Deanna did try to get some rest. She was exhausted—the whole crew was exhausted—but she could not fall asleep. She sat on the edge of her bed, then stood to pace the darkened room. As an empath, she had been trained from adolescence to put aside the troubles of others, but sometimes the troubles were so great that no one, however well trained, could sleep. She had felt a similar wakefulness many times, but this was odd. The *Enterprise* had not yet entered the system where Nunanavik awaited. She should not have been feeling anything but her own weariness and the regular troubles of the crew.

And yet she was. There had to be a reason.

She dressed quickly and left for the bridge. Data had the helm. When the turbolift doors opened, he turned to her, then stood. "Counselor Troi," he said.

Deanna thought that even the android looked tired. "Have we changed our ETA at Nunanavik?" she asked.

"No," he said. "We will enter orbit around the planet in two hours and thirty-eight minutes, exactly as estimated when we set course."

Was she just imagining what the people on Nunanavik were feeling?

"Is something wrong?" Data asked.

Deanna explained. "Have we learned anything new?"

"Very little. Twenty-three words, to be precise."

"Words?"

"Twelve ships leaving Nunanavik have passed within sensor and communication range. The ionized dust garbled their transmissions. The computer is attempting to sort out anything meaningful, but it has been able to decipher only twenty-three words from the static, none of them in context or—"

"What were those words?"

"From the first ship: *frostbitten, dying, cold;* from the second: *cold;* from the third, a phrase: *"Help them,"* and again the word *cold;* from the fourth—"

"Thank you, Data." That was it, Deanna thought. She was picking up the feelings of people lucky enough to be aboard ships *leaving* Nunanavik.

"Three more ships passing the *Enterprise,*" an ensign reported.

"Open all hailing frequencies," Data said. "Attempt to establish contact."

Any information the ships could provide might help them.

And Deanna sat down, almost overcome by the loss and heartbreak emanating from those crowded ships.

"All communications garbled as before," another ensign reported. "Computer attempting to decipher."

Data turned back to Deanna. "We will likely pass many more ships. Every available craft will certainly attempt exit before atmosphere collapse. Shall I order you a sedative from sickbay? You still have some time to sleep."

"No," Deanna said. "I don't think even a sedative could make me sleep now. I'm going back to the main shuttlebay. I'm sure the maintenance crews can use two more hands."

## ATMOSPHERE COLLAPSE: 5 HOURS, 23 MINUTES, 18 SECONDS

"Is that the best picture you can display?" Captain Picard asked.

The main viewer on the bridge showed a world shrouded in dust.

"No," Data said. "That is the actual view. I have programmed the computer to remove eighty-eight point seven percent of the dust from the image on screen. If we were to remove one hundred percent, the image would break up into inconsistent—"

"Put it on screen," Picard ordered.

The image before them was replaced with one much brighter. It showed a world blue and white with ice and snow. It was so bright that some people viewing it had to look away. Data shaded the brighter tones, and the light softened. "By now the temperature is cold enough that all the water vapor will have condensed out of the atmosphere," he said. "The snow and ice on the surface will be quite deep."

"How does this compare to images recorded before the dust cloud?" Picard asked.

Data entered commands into the computer. The main viewer

66

began to display older images, each darker than what they had been seeing, though they all looked icy and cold.

"It is now summer in Nunanavik's northern hemisphere," Data said. "As you know, arctic worlds such as this show little seasonal variation. Still, the difference between what was normal and what we are now seeing is striking. Here is the current image again."

The room visibly brightened.

"I calculate that ninety-eight point six percent of the surface is abnormally covered with snow or ice," Data said.

"At least the people down there know how to handle cold," Picard said.

"Not a temperature that freezes the atmosphere," Data said.

"We have audio and visual incoming from Nunanavik," Commander Riker announced.

"On screen, Number One," Picard said.

The image of a young Inuit woman wrapped in furs appeared before them. She was shivering. ". . . freezing, dying. Population down one third. We've called those left into the following sixteen settlements: Inuvik, Tanana, Anvik, Thule . . ."

Shortly after she finished sending the names, the message began to break up.

"Tell her help is on the way," Picard said. "Data, work that list of settlements into the evacuation plan. Riker, how long before we're ready to launch the shuttles?"

"Thirty-one minutes."

"Data, take the helm. Riker, Worf, Troi, La Forge, Crusher—to the conference lounge."

Deanna was finishing the final flight check of the cargo shuttle *Fossey*'s environmental systems when she got the call to the meeting. The air tanks were full, and she marked their status on the flight-check board before hurrying to the turbolift. Worf entered just ahead of her. He held the doors until she had stepped inside.

His pleasure at seeing her again lifted her spirits. The lift shot up toward the bridge.

"Did you get any sleep?" she asked.

"There is too much work to be done to sleep. I'll sleep afterward."

But Deanna wondered if any of them would be able to sleep "afterward." They all knew they wouldn't be able to save everyone on the planet. The doors opened, and Deanna and Worf hurried toward the conference lounge. Dr. Crusher entered just ahead of them.

Captain Picard was conferring with those who were already present. "La Forge, status report on the transporters. Can we use them?"

"No, sir," replied the chief engineer. "The dust cloud remains consistently thick. If we tried to transport through it, we'd lose matter-stream integrity."

He had been expecting that answer; nevertheless, Picard looked resigned. "We're almost finished stripping down the shuttles to make room for more people," the captain said. "Cargo shuttles can now carry fifty. Personnel shuttles, twelve—but people will have to stand. The *Calypso,* thirty."

They were depressingly low numbers, but it was the best they could do.

"Flight crew status, Riker," Picard said. "Everyone ready?"

"Pilots are flight-ready, but we're short one copilot," Riker said.

"Lieutenant Barretto is clinically exhausted," Dr. Crusher said. "I could not certify him."

"We're scrambling for a replacement," Riker said.

Deanna spoke up. "I've been studying shuttle-flight piloting in the holodeck, and I passed Level Four when we docked at Earth Station McKinley."

Level Four required fifty hours of actual shuttle flight. "More than enough for a copilot," Picard said.

"I'd be honored if she were to fly with me," Worf said.

"Make it so," the captain said. Picard, La Forge, and Riker were also on the roster of flight-ready pilots—just in case it became necessary to make immediate command-level decisions down on the planet's surface. Picard was flying the captain's yacht, the *Calypso*.

"Anything else?" Picard asked.

"Sir," Worf said. "The people on Nunanavik will fight to board shuttles. I advise sending armed guards."

Picard paused. Putting guards on the shuttles would mean fewer lives saved—but if the shuttles faced riots on the ground, even more would die. "See if you can assess on-ground security arrangements first," Picard said finally. "If communication is impossible, send two guards per shuttle."

Picard started for the door, then paused again. "Data?" he said.

"Sir," came Data's voice over the speakers.

"How many people are left to evacuate?"

"An exact figure is impossible to calculate."

"An estimate, then," Picard said, exasperation creeping into his voice.

"A conservative estimate would be in excess of eighty-two thousand."

Picard sighed. "Do your best, everyone." Then he left the room.

Contact with the ground was nearly impossible, and most of what did come through was unintelligible, so Worf made plans to send guards on the first flights down. He left the matter up to pilot discretion after that. If they found conditions secure, they could leave the guards behind on subsequent flights.

Worf hurried to dress in Federation cold-weather gear, then boarded the cargo shuttle *Goodall*, the shuttle he would fly. Deanna was already on board downloading their flight-path assignment. She looked up at him and smiled.

Worf froze for a moment in the doorway. Counselor Deanna Troi was a fellow officer, he told himself. She was his copilot on this mission. But none of that seemed to matter when she smiled at him.

Deanna had turned back to her work. She had set her coat and hat on the floor next to her seat. The sleeves were too bulky for her to work in comfortably. "We're headed for Anvik," she said. "A city on the second largest continent, ten degrees from the equator—a once balmy port city, by this world's standards."

Worf sat down. "How many people?" he asked.

"Data's best estimate is five thousand thirty-two."

Worf began running the preflight diagnostics, and Deanna performed her part flawlessly. "You have learned well," he told her.

"Thank you," she said.

Worf forced himself to concentrate. They finished their flight checks. He saw that the two security guards were in their seats. While they waited for liftoff clearance, he contacted Data on the bridge. "How many shuttles from other craft are you sending to Anvik?" he asked.

"Eight shuttles from the merchant ship *Hong Kong* will follow you in ten minutes," Data said. "I will assign others as they become available."

"Excellent," Worf said. "That gives us time to see to security arrangements on the ground before they arrive."

They were cleared for liftoff. Worf piloted the shuttle out of the bay and took it on a rapid descent to the surface.

Deanna did not question the steepness of their trajectory. The instruments showed everything within acceptable limits, if on the outer edge. The shuttle could take what Worf was doing to it.

She breathed deeply and looked at Worf. He was all work now. He gave piloting his full concentration. She ran her checks and called out the necessary statistics. Worf acknowledged them.

But one time she caught Worf looking at her—not at the instruments, not at the world rushing up toward them. She was glad they were working together. She knew Worf had genuine confidence in her and her training, but that wasn't the only reason he'd been eager to have her assigned as his copilot.

She smiled again.

Data worked with a calm fury to coordinate the evacuation. He and the crew on the bridge transmitted a steady stream of information to ships incoming and to the seventy-three ships already in orbit above Nunanavik. They had to set orbits, assign shuttles flight-path information, send detailed geographical data on Nunanavik that civilian craft might not routinely have, apportion shuttles to the settlements as fairly as possible, coordinate launch times and, shortly, begin tracking the first of the return flights. Flight safety was critical. With so many people to save, they had no room for error.

"Communication with outgoing shuttles from the *Enterprise,* the *Kolinahr,* and the *Raj Veda* is currently impossible," an ensign reported.

"Attempt to reestablish contact," Data said. "Scanners, track them."

Sixty-four percent of their communications were not getting through the ionized dust on the first try. Three crew members worked just to handle requests for retransmission of data. The communication breakdown meant unavoidable delays. Data could calculate how many lives each delay cost, but he did not complete those calculations. No one would have wanted to know. They were all doing the best they could.

"The *Tamilquara* reports it is carrying materials for two pressure domes that should withstand the collapse of the atmosphere. They have the crews and just enough time to assemble them."

"How many people can those domes hold?"

"Five thousand each, standing room only, six hours' air supply."

"Send them to Inuvik," Data said.

Practically everyone in Inuvik could crowd into those domes. Data wondered what else the merchant ships might be carrying that was capable of saving lives. He assigned a team to begin making inquiries.

"Shuttles from the *Hong Kong* launched nine point five minutes ahead of schedule, sir!" an ensign reported.

Data looked up. An early launch was dangerous, given the crowded skies. "Calculate flight paths. Transmit corrections, if necessary."

"Those shuttles are coming down hard behind the *Calypso* and the *Enterprise* shuttles *Hawking* and *Goodall!*"

"Order them to pull back!" Data said. "Contact the *Hong Kong* and get them to help, too."

The crew rushed to complete those tasks. Data himself transmitted warnings to the *Enterprise* shuttles. He tried everything to reach them. Nothing worked.

The bridge grew quiet for a moment.

None of the shuttles from the *Hong Kong* was pulling back. The *Enterprise* shuttles were not beginning evasive maneuvers. None of them had received the warnings.

Data stood as the scanners tracked the flight paths, which were clearly merging. The eight shuttles from the *Hong Kong* would come down right on top of the *Enterprise* shuttles. The ensign at the scanners held onto her console as if bracing for impact.

Worf eased his shuttle into Nunanavik's freezing atmosphere, then plunged it down toward the surface. He hoped to shave two minutes off their ETA in Anvik, and all indications were that he'd do that and more. There was no turbulence to interfere with their flight. Movement of the air had mostly stopped. The moisture had condensed out of the atmosphere, and there were no clouds. The clear sky was streaked with tiny flashes of red as dust showered down around them and burned.

It was an eerie sky to fly through.

All twenty of the *Enterprise* shuttles and the *Calypso* flew together to a point above a major plateau, then split off to their destinations. Worf flew due south, in formation with the *Hawking* and the *Calypso*. They gained altitude again to cross a jagged coastal mountain range cut with deep canyons and passes and scoured by massive glaciers. The land rushing past below them was a patchwork of white snow and blue ice.

Suddenly an alarm rang out, and red light filled the shuttle.

"Eight ships incoming!" Deanna shouted.

"Attempting evasive maneuvers," Worf said, and he guided the shuttle down into a deep canyon.

But the incoming ships were all around them, ahead of them, above them.

Deanna rushed to transmit correct flight-path information. "Pull back! Pull back!" she shouted, hailing the incoming shuttles. "Correct your courses!"

The transmissions from the incoming shuttles were a confusion of panicked chatter.

"This can't be right!"

"Where did these mountains come from! There weren't supposed to be mountains!"

*"Enterprise* shuttles dead ahead!"

"Pull up!"

"Dump speed!"

Something hit the *Goodall*. Worf and Deanna watched a merchant's shuttle slam against the far canyon wall and explode. Their shuttle began to spin down toward the canyon floor.

Worf struggled to regain control, but the ice and snow rushed up at frightening speed. The shuttle shook so badly that Deanna thought it would break apart, but gradually the spinning stopped, and slowly the ship began to respond. Deanna started a damage assessment, checked fuel supplies and cabin pressure. She tried to think if there was something she should have done to prevent the crash. She wanted to ask Worf, but this was not the time.

Their flight leveled out close above the canyon floor. Neither Deanna nor Worf looked back at the snowstorm the shuttle was raising in its wake. Neither spoke. Slowly the shuttle gained altitude. The two guards on board with them cheered when it cleared the canyon rim—but the shuttle was not gaining altitude fast enough to clear the mountain pass ahead.

"We will have to abandon ship," Worf said. He could see that they were going to slam into the mountain. "Guards, put on your paragliders." By the time he finished issuing the order, the guards were already putting their arms through the shoulder straps on the devices that would enable them to coast down to the planet surface.

Seconds later, Worf shouted, "Jump!" He hit the button that blew the hatch open. An immediate blast of freezing air made them all choke.

The guards jumped. The white wings of their paragliders immediately expanded to a span of six meters, stable and graceful.

"Jump, Deanna!" Worf shouted as he eased the shuttle over a small ridge, buying them a little more time.

But Deanna was scrambling to grab her coat—which she didn't think about until she was exposed to the frigid atmosphere, and which had slid some distance away from her seat. Worf pulled on another paraglider, grabbed Deanna in his arms, and leaped through the hatch just in time.

The shuttle exploded against the mountainside. Shrapnel battered Worf and Deanna and their paraglider. Their fall seemed to go on and on, across ridges and down through a deepening valley. They slammed into a snowbank at the base of a glacier.

When they stopped tumbling, Worf thought two things: *I am*

*alive,* and *I did not let go of Deanna.* She was limp in his arms, but he could feel her breathing.

Picard held Deanna's charred coat and stared at the burning wreckage of the *Goodall.* He'd ordered the other shuttles to continue on, then circled back to rescue any survivors of the crash, picking up the two security guards. But he found no sign of Worf or Deanna. The *Enterprise* could not detect them—which could be just dust interference, Picard tried to tell himself. But most of the downed shuttle was still burning. They could not get near it.

And here was Deanna's coat.

There were no signs of life.

Picard was not certain that he could make himself move, but move he did. He and the guards boarded the *Calypso* and circled the area again and again, but they found no sign of Worf or Deanna. It did not appear that they had jumped. The two rescued guards told how desperate the situation had been, how little time they'd had before impact.

There was only one logical conclusion.

Picard left the crash scene, still carrying Deanna's coat.

Worf and Deanna had been hit again and again with shrapnel from the explosion. Worf did his best to stop their bleeding. Then he broke apart the paraglider and used pieces of the frame to set Deanna's broken right arm. Shrapnel had torn so many holes in the paraglider's wings that he wondered how it had flown as far as it had.

Deanna was freezing without her coat and hat. He picked her up, tucked her inside his coat as much as he could, and started up the mountain. Shrapnel had ripped holes in his coat and torn off his communicator. Deanna's communicator had been attached to her coat. They had no way of calling for help, nothing to do but climb up to the smoking crash site. There lay their best hope of being picked up. He hurried on.

## ATMOSPHERE COLLAPSE:
## 3 HOURS, 6 MINUTES, 17 SECONDS

Worf did not know when the three old women had come to them on the mountainside. He sat in their igloo and tried to remember, but could not. All of a sudden they had been there; they had taken Deanna out of his arms and carried her for him, and they had brought them here.

One of the women put a cup of something hot in his hands. Worf sipped the buttery liquid. "My name is Amalik," the woman said. "My friends are Nenana and Ilingnorak. I've rescued many people from freezing before, but never a Klingon."

"I thank you for what you have done," Worf said. He looked at his watch and saw how little time they had. The women had no communicators, so he and Deanna still had to get up to the crash site. He watched the women wrap Deanna in a seal-fur parka and dress her in leggings. Worf thought she looked more beautiful than ever with her black hair contrasted against the white seal fur.

"We saw your ship coming down," Nenana said.

"Then we heard it crash, and we saw the smoke," Amalik offered.

"A different shuttle landed shortly after and took off again," added Nenana.

"What?" Worf said. He set down the cup, and he was ashamed when he felt his hands trembling. "You saw a shuttle land and leave?" he asked.

The women nodded.

"Have other shuttles returned to the crash site?"

All of them shook their heads.

He and Deanna had been abandoned for dead, Worf knew. Soon they would indeed be dead. "How far are we from Anvik?" he asked.

"Eight kilometers," said Nenana.

Worf picked up the cup and finished the warm liquid in a gulp. "We must go," he said. "We have little time."

But the women just sat there.

"Don't you know what's happening?" Worf asked.

"Of course we know," Ilingnorak said, speaking for the first time. "But you can't rescue everyone—there aren't enough ships. We're old, Klingon. We built this igloo with our hands, and we are waiting together to die."

Worf was quiet for a moment. "I admire your courage," he said finally, "but I could never wait for death like this. I would fight to live."

"Oh, to be young again and believe that life itself is reason enough for living!" Ilingnorak said.

Worf thought about that. More than people would die here, he knew. A way of life would end.

Deanna stirred. Worf helped her sit up. Amalik pressed a cup of water to her lips. Deanna coughed. "Where are we?" she asked, and Worf explained. He held Deanna in his arms and turned to the women.

"Give me the route to Anvik," he said. "We have to try to get there."

The women did the best they could without a map. They spoke the directions; then they drew the route in charcoal on the ice of the igloo floor.

"You will never find the way," Ilingnorak said.

"Then we'll die in the attempt," Worf said. He put on his coat and started to pull Deanna across the igloo floor toward the entrance.

"I'll take you," Amalik said. "You'll never make it otherwise."

"I'll go, too," Nenana said.

Ilingnorak was quiet for a short time. "I did not want to die in a metal building," she said, "but I'll go, too. Worse than dying there would be dying here alone."

Worf waited a minute in the igloo entrance while the women prepared for the trip. They gave Deanna and Worf scraps of caribou skin to put over their noses and mouths. Breathing through the skin was smelly, but necessary, Worf knew. They had to protect their lungs. There would be air to breathe after it was too cold for anyone to survive—oxygen would be the third gas to freeze, after carbon dioxide and ozone—but breathing it was going to get harder and harder.

Each of the women carried spears made from caribou bone. "For bears," Amalik said. "They were endangered on Earth. We gave them a second home here, but our kindness didn't change their nature."

Amalik and Nenana hoisted Deanna to a standing position and supported her with their arms. "You go ahead to break trail," Ilingnorak said to Worf. "Straight ahead, between those two rocks."

Worf trudged forward, but soon looked back and realized he was outdistancing the women. They were not strong enough to travel as fast as he could, and Deanna was in no shape to walk, even with assistance. Worf paced back to the women and lifted Deanna into his arms.

It was going to be a long eight kilometers.

Picard stamped for a moment in the warmth of the captain's yacht docking bay on deck sixteen, while maintenance crews rushed to prepare the *Calypso* for a return trip. Picard had brought a load of children from Thule, including three from the hospital there. Those three were being rushed to sickbay.

Beverly Crusher was supervising the patient transfer. Picard looked at her and knew that she knew. He supposed that Data had told her about Worf and Deanna. She touched his arm briefly. Neither of them said anything—but then, what is there to say? Picard wondered.

## ATMOSPHERE COLLAPSE:
## 1 HOUR, 43 MINUTES, 37 SECONDS

Deanna drifted in and out of consciousness, but while conscious she knew she was in Worf's arms. She could taste blood on her lips, and quickly realized it was coming from her nose. The moisture was gone from the air, and as a result they all had nosebleeds. She watched Worf's breath pushing out the caribou skin around his nose and mouth when he exhaled, and she saw a slow trickle of blood run along the lower edge of the skin. A drop fell now and then onto her white seal parka. "Was it me, Worf?" she asked.

"What?"

"Did I do something to cause the crash?"

He walked a few steps before answering. "No," he said. "I will ask for you again when I next fly a shuttle."

Deanna knew he was telling the truth, and she felt relieved. "I can walk now," she said.

Worf set her down and helped her stand, then stood breathing heavily beside her.

*What a burden I've become,* she thought.

"We can't stop," Ilingnorak said. "Go ahead, Worf. We'll help Deanna walk. The way is downhill straight on, around that rock outcrop."

Deanna walked until she thought she'd pass out again, then she walked some more. After a time, she awakened and realized she had passed out. Worf was carrying her again.

Worf rushed ahead, breaking trail, listening to the women's directions. He estimated they had covered only five kilometers so far. When they came to a steep embankment, Worf climbed it and put Deanna down on the crest; then he pulled up each of the Inuit women. All of them rested briefly, gasping for air. The cold when they weren't moving was painful, and it hurt to breathe. Worf pulled out his phaser and fired it at a rock alongside the trail. It soon glowed red and radiated heat. The snow and ice around it melted, creating a' puddle of water that would soon freeze solid again. The women hurried ahead and huddled around the rock.

They had to rest, frigid atmosphere or no. Worf knew even he had to catch his breath. He carried Deanna to the rock and sat her down on one side of it. Just a few minutes, and they would be on the move again. . . .

None of them heard it coming. Suddenly in the dim light, barely discernible against the snow, Worf saw something white and huge rushing toward them.

Polar bear.

Worf drew his phaser, fired too quickly, and hit snow. He fired again and hit the bear—but the creature was not fazed. It stood on its back legs and roared. Amalik and Ilingnorak threw their spears. Amalik's hit the bear in the stomach, but the point barely grazed its flesh. Worf adjusted his phaser to a higher setting, hoping that being hit with a stronger charge would make the bear decide to go away.

The women crowded behind him. Worf fired again, and this time the bear was hurt. It sank back down onto all fours. With a growl, it swatted at the spear sticking out of its stomach, dislodging it, then lumbered away into the snow where none of them could see it.

Amalik ran to retrieve her spear.

"The bear will come for us again," Ilingnorak said. "It is the way of bears. They do not give up."

"I will kill it, then," Worf said, and he reset his phaser a second time.

The air was noticeably colder than it had been a short time earlier. Blood had frozen on all their lips. Worf pulled Deanna to her feet. "Hurry!" he told everyone. "And keep watch for the bear."

## ATMOSPHERE COLLAPSE: 57 MINUTES, 23 SECONDS

They came to a flat plain, the beginning of a short stretch of relatively easy terrain that remained between themselves and Anvik. The plain was covered with unbroken snowdrifts. It was late afternoon, almost dark, but the way ahead was clear. The snow and ice would shine even after sunset.

Worf knew Deanna was getting weaker all the time, perhaps going into shock from her broken arm and shrapnel wounds. The women did not stop talking to Deanna. They all tried to keep her walking when she could, keep her talking, keep her going. Worf wondered if with all their talking the women were convincing themselves—if they were finding reasons to hope for life again. It would be cruel if their new hope and his words about not waiting for death went for naught. He knew how limited shuttle space was, but he swore that if they made it to Anvik in time, he would find a way to save these women.

"Do you know how the stars came to be?" Ilingnorak asked Deanna.

She did not answer right away. "Clouds of hydrogen atoms get compressed by—I can't remember what," she said. "Something compresses clouds of atoms—"

"No! No. My grandmother from Earth told me it was like this: The first man and woman had six children, and polar bears hunted them. The Raven had not yet created the caribou or the seals, so there was nothing for the bears to eat but People. Whenever the man and woman thought they had found a safe place, the bears would find them, and the People had to fight them off. One by one, the bears ate the children: first the oldest boy, then two girls, then the youngest boy. Now there was only one boy and one girl left, and the first People had nowhere to hide. The bears circled the fire that night, wanting to eat the last two children. The mother became so angry that she scooped up ashes and coals from the fire and threw them at the bears. She threw them so hard, the bears were knocked into the black night sky where the coals grew and became stars, and the ashes became worlds around the stars. The People went out to hide on those worlds from the bears that still hunt us in the night."

"Star bears found this world and are taking it," Amalik said.

## ATMOSPHERE COLLAPSE:
## 43 MINUTES, 10 SECONDS

Data had found a way to save over five hundred more lives. Two mining supply ships carried emergency-escape domes designed to fit over exits from mining shafts on asteroids and protect four people for thirty minutes. Data extended the thirty minutes to two hours with oxygen canisters from another ship. He located portable heaters on four other ships. He had one hundred forty domes, extra oxygen for each, plus eighty heaters, and he had started sending the equipment down to the surface. The shuttle pilots could rescue the people in the domes even after the atmosphere had collapsed.

"Incoming from Captain Picard," an ensign reported. Picard was returning to the *Enterprise* with his third load of refugees.

"On screen," Data said.

After a moment, the grainy image of the captain's face displayed on the main viewer. "The Oceanographic Institute in Thule has one submarine capable of carrying forty people. It's just set out with fifty-one for an undersea volcanic vent in hopes that the sea won't freeze there quickly. Transmitting coordinates of the vent. Use scanners to track them, if you can. We'll try to pull them out after atmosphere collapse."

Data quickly calculated the thickness of the ice they'd have to blast through. It would be hard, but not impossible. He explained about the mining domes to Picard.

"How many people have been lifted up so far?" Picard asked.

"Forty-five thousand two hundred thirty-one," Data said.

Worf struggled to the top of a gentle rise—and there before them shone the lights of Anvik, bright against the dark sky. The women crowded up around him; then they all walked briskly for the city.

"When we met the bear," Worf said, "you did not act like women who want to die."

"We did not," Amalik admitted.

"We are not fighting now just to save you and Deanna," Iling-norak said.

And they did not seem like women who wanted to die. Worf suddenly realized they never had been. They'd just been giving their places to the young.

## ATMOSPHERE COLLAPSE: 15 MINUTES, 12 SECONDS

There was a shuttle from the *Enterprise* in Anvik. Deanna could sense its presence. Even she was moving quickly now, Worf pulling her along at his side. She did her best to keep up. It was downhill now all the way into Anvik. She wanted to live so badly—and they were so close. Surely they'd make it.

Geordi La Forge stood back while people crowded onto the shuttle. They were trying to take at least one parent of each child who had been sent ahead on earlier flights. There was not enough space for both parents to go. Geordi looked away—the scene was too painful. He stamped his cold feet and scanned the frozen ocean. He looked up at the sky, and it was still there, for now, but not as clear as it had been. Trails of vapor misted high up: freezing carbon dioxide, he realized. He turned and looked out beyond the city—and saw a small group of people about two hundred meters away moving in his direction.

"Shuttle's full," one of the guards said.

Geordi gazed into the distance—and recognized Worf and Deanna with three Inuit women!

"Hold the doors!" he shouted.

Geordi rushed toward the group to meet them partway. "I thought you were dead!" he said.

They never stopped moving. Geordi took Deanna's other arm and helped Worf trot toward the shuttle with her.

"Why are all these people still here?" one of the women shouted from behind them.

"The only shuttle's full!" Geordi shouted.

The women stopped. And then Worf stopped.

"We have to go!" Geordi shouted.

"I give my place to one of you," Worf told the women.

"Go!" Ilingnorak shouted at him. "You are young—life itself is reason enough for living!"

The women sat in the snow and held onto each other. Tendrils of frozen carbon dioxide vapor were swirling around the snow-drifts away from the heat of the city.

Geordi explained that another shuttle had brought down some mining domes, and the domes were being given out inside the spaceport terminal. "See if you can get one," he told the women. "We'll pick you up on our next trip." He ran for the shuttle, pulling Deanna with him.

Worf walked back and drew Ilingnorak to her feet. "You rescued a Klingon from freezing to death," he told her. "I will not leave you to freeze now. Come with me—all of you!" And he ran for the terminal, pulling Ilingnorak after him. Amalik and Nenana ran behind them.

Once more he was giving them hope, Worf thought.

Once more he hoped it wasn't mere cruelty.

"Worf!" Geordi shouted from the shuttle doorway. Deanna was already inside.

"Go!" Worf shouted back. "I am helping these women!"

Geordi turned, and the shuttle doors closed.

Worf let go of Ilingnorak and ran as hard as he could to the terminal doorway. Hundreds of people milled about, most having resigned themselves to their fates. A few were going after the mining domes, reasoning that the scant hope they offered was better than none. Worf shoved his way inside the terminal and took a dome and an oxygen canister.

"We have no heaters left!" the woman behind the counter shouted at him. "You'll freeze inside that dome."

"I will take my chances," he said. He rushed back outside to where the Inuit women were waiting for him.

He burned away a small circle of snow in an explosion of steam that dusted them in frost. He shoved the escape dome down onto the rock and set it off. The seal melted against the rock, making an airtight enclosure. Worf opened the hatch, and heat from the sealing process rushed out. Worf pulled aside the caribou skin and breathed in a lungful of the heated air.

"Get inside quickly," Worf ordered the women.

Nenana started crawling through the hatch. Someone set off a dome near theirs, and it sputtered and steamed on the surface but did not create a seal.

"Find a rock we can heat with my phaser," Worf told Amalik, and he ran to the dome that had not sealed. "Stand back," he told the people there. The air was misty with carbon dioxide vapor. He fired his phaser at the seal and melted it against the rock. He walked slowly around the dome, firing carefully to create a seal without puncturing the dome. By the time he finished, he could hardly breathe. But he hurried to another dome having trouble and sealed it for the people there.

Amalik tossed a rock into their dome and crawled inside. She called out for Worf.

For a moment he could not move. He gasped for air, feeling as though every breath was ripping at his lungs. He willed his legs toward his dome, ignoring the pain that came from them. He kicked the hatch, Ilingnorak opened it, and he fell into the opening.

The women pulled him inside and sealed the hatch. Worf could not move. "Use my phaser to heat the rock," he said hoarsely.

Ilingnorak took the phaser and fired it at the rock. It soon glowed, but the heat from it could not entirely drive back the cold.

"My back is freezing," Nenana said.

Worf watched the women turn their backs to the heat, then turn around to face it, then turn their backs to it again. After a moment, he sat up and held his hands over the rock. He leaned his face down over it.

"I can't get warm," Nenana said.

The floor of the shelter, which rested only inches above the ground, grew colder and colder. Worf wished they had a covering to put on it.

Amalik and Nenana were both crying now and rubbing themselves vigorously. Worf heated the rock again. "We are all suffering," he said. "But we must calm ourselves to conserve air."

The women made themselves stop crying. When they were quiet, Amalik spoke softly. "The star bears are coming for us," she said.

"We will fight them," Worf replied.

They had heated the rock so many times that it had cracked in two, and part of it had melted down into the floor of the dome. Still, they kept it glowing. In addition to the heat, it provided a bit of light; outside the dome, the sun had set. After a time, they heard a soft patter against the dome, then a hard rain. Ozone, Worf knew. The rain let up, but after ten minutes it began again. Rain slammed against the dome in a galestorm. Oxygen, this time.

Ilingnorak held his hand. "You are brave, Klingon," she said. "And loyal—all the best things I've read about your people."

Worf said nothing. They listened to the oxygen rain. After a time, Ilingnorak spoke again. "You love her," she said. "And surely she will love you. That makes us all happy."

Worf checked their supply of air. He heated the rock again. He listened to the gases of the atmosphere rain down in the darkness and freeze around them.

*Love Deanna?* he wondered.

What other name was there for what he felt?

## ATMOSPHERE: COLLAPSED

It was an *Enterprise* shuttle that came for them. Worf listened to the crew open domes and rescue the people near them. He listened to the crunch of footsteps around their dome. He heard them burn away the layers of gassy ice above their hatch and attach a crawl tube. He listened for the hatch on the shuttle end to open, and the slam of it echoed down the tube. Then their hatch twisted open.

"Hurry! This way!" a man said, and he began crawling away, back toward the shuttle.

"We need help!" Worf called.

The man recognized the familiar voice. He came back and shone a light into the dome. "Lieutenant Worf!" he shouted. Then he called back to the shuttle on his communicator: "I've found Worf!"

The man extended his arms into the dome to help its occupants get into the tube. Worf helped Nenana up, then Amalik. Ilingnorak kissed Worf and crawled after her friends. Worf followed them all.

For two days, Worf could not move. Dr. Crusher had to regenerate forty percent of his lungs. His throat and the lining of his nostrils were also damaged. He had frostbite on his feet, hands, and face, but Dr. Crusher thought it would leave few scars.

But Worf had other scars, not visible. As he lay in his bed, he kept thinking about the people who hadn't gotten into domes. He felt a deep sorrow for them, even as he respected them for their courage in the face of death. He did not know if he would ever be able to forget the sacrifices of the brave people of Nunanavik.

Dr. Crusher helped Deanna to Worf's side on the second day. "How many times did you save my life?" Deanna asked him. She leaned down and kissed his forehead. "Thank you," she whispered.

Worf held onto her hand. After she left, he touched the place where Deanna had kissed him.

Picard visited Worf each day of his recovery. On the first day, he looked at the bandages from the frostbite and the stitches that closed the shrapnel wounds on Worf's neck and face, and he realized those were only the dressings and stitches he could see. "You are hurt, my friend," Picard said.

*I am hurting,* Worf thought, *but not in the way you imagine.* He quieted his thoughts of those who had died, and then found himself able to talk. "These wounds are nothing," he said.

Picard was quiet for a time. "I've met Amalik, Nenana, and Ilingnorak," he said. "They are healing, and should live. From what Ilingnorak tells me, you will figure prominently in Inuit legend, if she has anything to say about it."

Worf allowed himself a slight smile, though it hurt to move his face like that. "Those women would be a credit to any people," he said.

"I am proud they are descended from Earth," Picard said.

"When we are healed, I will let them know how I honor them."

"I think they know," Picard said. "How could they not?"

After a time, Picard left. The crew of the *Enterprise* could rest now. They had done everything possible. The crew of the *Carpathia* was bringing up the ten thousand people in the pressure domes. Another ship was implementing a plan to rescue the people in the submarine. The *Enterprise* waited in case its tired crew needed to provide emergency assistance. Data calculated that their combined efforts had saved more than sixty-five thousand lives.

In a few days, Dr. Crusher removed the dressings from Worf's hands. Now that he was able to touch and feel with his hands again, Worf found his thoughts drifting back to when he had held Deanna in his arms.

She had felt so small. . . . When they'd been falling in the paraglider, he had hung on to her so tightly he'd been afraid she would break. That she had felt small and fragile surprised him, because she had always seemed so strong. Her strength was what originally had attracted him to her, after all. But her strength did not come from her stature. He thought of the Inuit women. Stature—or youth—did not give them strength, either. They had neither of those.

But they had something more important, or rather they understood something more important. Ilingnorak had told him in

88

Anvik to go on for two reasons: first, because he was young. But Worf thought that, where life was concerned, age did not matter. What mattered was the second reason. It was what had given the women hope again and again. It was what had given the people left in Anvik the courage to crawl into the domes and struggle to live.

Life itself is reason enough for living.

It always is, Worf thought. Young or old, it always is.

# A Night at Sandrine's

## By Christie Golden

**STARDATE 50396.2**

*The cool, briny scent of the sea floated through the damp air. Mist clung to the stone buildings and made the cobblestone of the old streets slick with moisture. The golden glow of lamps gleamed faintly through the fog to guide the wanderer home, and as he opened the door, the welcoming sounds of laughter and music wafted out to greet him. All was warmth and good humor here, especially tonight.*

*He stood in the doorway, savoring the moment. Yvette was performing "La vie en rose," her red mouth curving about the words and quivering ever so slightly. Smells of smoke from the crackling fire, of perfume and of good food made him smile. Though a woman owned the establishment, in a sense, this place truly belonged to him. Whatever their rank outside these doors might be, he knew: Sooner or later, everyone came to Sandrine's.*

*He adjusted his fedora and brought the cigarette to his lips. The tip flared orange as he inhaled, and—*

"You're puffing your carrot."

"What?" Lieutenant Tom Paris was startled out of his reverie by the sound of B'Elanna Torres's voice.

The half-Klingon chief engineer grinned up at him. "Your carrot," she repeated, indicating the carrot stick he held in his hand. She mimed bringing it to her lips and inhaling from it. "You were doing this?"

Paris felt himself blush. "Oh. Guess I just got caught up in the moment." Deliberately, he popped the vegetable into his mouth and crunched on it.

And a hell of a moment it was. Captain Janeway had yielded to Paris's request for an old-fashioned party in the holodeck, specifically program Paris 3—a French bistro called Chez Sandrine. *Voyager* was presently traveling through a very long and very boring stretch of the Nekrit Expanse, and Paris had capitalized on the crew's restlessness. Together with Neelix, the self-appointed "morale officer," they had convinced Janeway that a party was just what the doctor ordered.

Taking it a step further, Paris had suggested it be a costume party. Most had agreed. Tom saw fedoras and trench coats, suits and canes, and uplifted hairdos and hats with netting—all right out of Earth's mid-20th century.

"Yes!" exclaimed Harry Kim as he sank the eight ball. He looked very young and innocent in tweed trousers, crisp white shirt, and red suspenders. Gaunt Gary, the resident pool shark Paris had recreated, feigned resignation.

"Pay up." Harry extended his hand as Gary sighed and handed over a fistful of holographic money.

Paris knew what was coming. "Rematch? I'd like to get some o' that green stuff back," said Gary.

"Oh, you bet, but I'll just take your money again," enthused Kim, already racking the balls.

"Harry, Harry, Harry," sighed Paris, shaking his head as he moved toward a small table by the fire. "He ought to know better. Gary's gonna fleece him."

"You know," said B'Elanna, slipping into the chair opposite Paris, "I'm surprised Chakotay agreed to this, after your last adventure with gambling."

"Ah, Chakotay's not so tough. Neelix and I swore that all the gambling proceeds would go right back into the replicator to provide some decent food for the party." With an extravagant wave, he indicated the lavish buffet, of which other crewmembers were eagerly partaking.

"Think he'll show up tonight?" she asked.

Tom shrugged. Sandrine was chatting with some other customers, and he flagged down Neelix, who was acting as maitre d' for the evening. The Talaxian grinned and ambled over toward them. He looked surprisingly debonair in the formal black-and-white tuxedo. Paris guessed he'd waxed his whiskers.

"Chakotay?" said Tom. "I don't know. Don't know if we'll see the Captain, either. They're kind of like your mom and dad sometimes, you know? 'You kids have your party, but don't stay up too late.' "

Neelix, who was pouring small glasses of port for each of them, laughed a little. "I hadn't thought about it that way, but I suppose you're right. Monsieur Paris, Mademoiselle Torres, here you are—a lovely port, replicated especially for the occasion."

"Thanks, Neelix," said B'Elanna. She brought the glass to her lips; then her eyes widened slightly. "Hey, boys. Mom's here."

Neelix followed her gaze. "My, my. I don't know about you two, but *my* mother never looked like that."

Paris, who was searching the room for one particular person, idly glanced toward the entrance of the bistro. And nearly spilled his wine.

Captain Janeway had, in every sense of the word, let her hair down. The red-brown mass tumbled about her bare shoulders, caught up on one side with a jeweled pin that reflected the mischievous sparkle in her blue eyes. Her floor-length gown of black satin clung to her slim figure in a most flattering fashion, but there was no hint of anything but elegance and class about her. The room fell silent. Janeway lifted her chin and smiled.

"Caesar has arrived," she announced. "Let the games begin!"

Approving laughter and a smattering of applause followed her statement. Grinning broadly, Janeway swept into the room and picked up a cue with the familiarity of one who knew the game well.

"Excuse me, but I shouldn't keep such a lovely lady waiting. Especially when the lady is our captain," said Neelix, hastening to Janeway with a glass of port already poured.

Paris was pleased. Not only had his captain actually showed up, but she was clearly getting into the spirit of things. Now if only another certain someone would show—

And there she was, standing in the entrance and looking about hesitantly. She was a stunning brunette, with carefully coiffed hair, chocolate brown eyes, wearing an elegantly tailored suit. There wasn't a woman in the place who could touch her for sultry dark good looks.

Ricky. The one constant in every holographic program Tom Paris had ever designed. She had appeared as the gentle damsel in distress in a knights-in-shining-armor scenario, a sexy Orion slave girl in another, and was the innocent American Abroad here in Sandrine's.

"Excuse me, my date is here," Tom said to B'Elanna. Eagerly, he rose and started to head in Ricky's direction when the bistro's owner, Sandrine, stopped him. She gazed up at him, her eyes cold and angry.

"Where were you last night?" she asked.

He shrugged. "That was so long ago I don't remember."

"Will I see you tonight?"

"I never make plans that far in advance." Sandrine was an extremely attractive older woman, and Tom was more than familiar with her charms. Tonight, though, he was in the mood for passive adoration, not Sandrine's tigerish loveplay. The jealous French-woman had once sneered at Ricky, calling her a "little puppy dog." Tom had replied that he wouldn't have Ricky any other way. She would be the icing on the cake to his triumph tonight. It was all going exactly as he planned.

Ricky had stepped inside and was heading toward the bar. Tom, smiling, sneaked up behind her and playfully put his hands over her eyes.

"Guess—"

He never made it to "who." The next thing he knew he was flat on his back, gasping for air like a fish, and staring up into Ricky's furious face. Conversation had stopped, and Paris, mortified, realized two things: Ricky—pretty, passive Ricky—had *thrown* him, and everyone had seen it.

He rose slowly, dusting himself off, and searched frantically for the least embarrassing way out of this confusing scenario.

He found it. "Excellent," Paris said with false heartiness. "You've mastered the throw even when you weren't expecting to have to use it. Everyone, give the lady a hand, she's spent a lot of time practicing self-defense!"

He started the applause. Others joined in, unsure what was going on. Paris caught Yvette's eye, gesticulated, and she immediately launched into *"Les amants d'un jour."* The other crewmembers turned back to their drinks, pool games, or conversation. Thank God, he was out of the spotlight for the moment. He wiped his face. It was wet. The movement made his back ache.

"Who the hell are you?" snapped Ricky. Her rumbling, sultry voice held no hint of teasing.

"Honey—" Paris moved forward placatingly, but she stepped backward just as quickly.

"Don't touch me again," she warned. "I asked you a question."

Paris gaped. "Ricky, don't you know me? It's Tom, sweetheart,

Tommy boy." He reached to touch her, to bring his face down to hers. "Perhaps this'll jog your memory."

Her slap almost bruised him. "I'm getting out of this—Sandrine! What kind of a place are you running these days?"

*"Certainement,* I am not sure I know myself," answered Sandrine, impaling Paris with her gaze. "It would appear that just *anybody* thinks he can wander into *my* bistro."

Tom's pleasant evening was rapidly unraveling. He glanced, utterly nonplussed, from Ricky to Sandrine. Normally, they reserved their glares for one another and treated him with sweet eyes and soft lips. Now, they had adopted almost mirrored poses—arms crossed, eyes hard and angry.

"Please observe the series of events," said a slightly strident voice that Paris didn't recognize. He turned to look at the speaker. She was petite but stood ramrod straight. Every strand of brown hair was in place, her makeup was perfect, her clothing suited to the occasion without being in the least remarkable. Her mouth and nose had a slightly pinched look to them. Tom figured her for somewhere in her forties.

The Doctor stood beside the woman, looking, as usual, rather pleased with himself. The woman continued.

"This . . . person—I hardly think he can be called a gentleman—brazenly approaches, *from behind,* a woman with whom he is unacquainted. When, understandably startled, she reacts instinctively to defend herself, he does not admit that he was in the wrong but instead invents a story to hide his shame. He then continues his pursuit of her without even bothering to properly introduce himself or apologize. He attempts an intimacy which would be improper in a public place under *any* circumstance and is justly reprimanded." The woman turned her piercing gaze to Ricky. "Bravo, Mademoiselle. He is a scoundrel and does not deserve you."

"Who the hell are you?" demanded Paris, echoing Ricky's earlier question. His face was red, but with anger this time.

"Note the demand. He fails to observe any sort of etiquette." The harridan turned to the Doctor. "I do hope that your situation has not deteriorated to such a level."

"Not at all," the Doctor replied. "I am merely a diamond in need of polishing. Mr. Paris, I fear, hasn't even been chipped out of the rock yet. Mr. Paris, may I present Etta. Etta, dear, this is Lieutenant Thomas Eugene Paris. He's *Voyager*'s pilot."

Etta extended a hand. "Charmed," she said in a voice that indicated she was anything but.

Recovering slightly, Tom bent over the gloved hand, kissed it quickly, and bowed. "A pleasure," he lied.

She raised an eyebrow. "Somewhat better."

"At Kes's suggestion, I've created a holographic character whom I have programmed with every nuance of human etiquette," the Doctor explained. "I thought perhaps this might help me become more efficient in dealing with my patients. Kes seems to think I'm lacking in that area."

"Kes's comments implied no criticism, and you have slighted her," reprimanded the etiquette program. "If we see her this evening, I suggest you apologize."

"See? It's working beautifully." He smirked a little.

"She going to tell us which wine to serve at your memorial service when I delete your program?" Tom smiled. Charmingly. He took perverse pleasure in the nasty looks both the Doctor and Etta shot him before they made their way to their table.

Tom watched them go. He wondered if he could bribe Neelix into spilling red wine on Etta's white blouse. Dismissing the thought, he turned again to Ricky.

She was gone.

"Having a bad night?" It was Torres.

"Uh, yeah, you could say that. B'Elanna," he went on, turning to her, "has there been any problem with the holodeck recently? Any, I don't know, unexpected surges of energy, something like that?"

She frowned. Her ridged brow furrowed even more than usual. "Not that I'm aware of."

Paris rubbed the small of his back. He thought about dragging the Doctor away from his supercilious date and getting the twinge treated, then dismissed the idea. The Doctor would refuse, on the grounds that the pain was deserved, and merely score another point with Etta. He'd just let the pain of the throw work its way out.

"I don't get it," he said, more to himself than Torres. "Usually when she's mad at me she . . . ."

"She what?" prompted Torres. She was grinning up at him in an almost malevolent fashion.

"You're enjoying this, aren't you?"

She shrugged. Belatedly, he realized that she, too, had dressed for the occasion. Torres wore a fashionable white and blue suit-dress with white pumps and a broad-brimmed hat. Her hair was styled, and she even sported dangly diamond earrings. Almost absently, he acknowledged that she looked good. Great, in fact.

"When your buddy Gaunt Gary over there gave me some line about treating tramps like ladies and vice versa, I said he was a pig and you were too, for designing him."

"So you did."

"Can I help it if I think it's funny that now you're getting a little muddy?"

He'd taken B'Elanna's gibing before, often, and almost as often admitted that she had a point. Now, though, anger rose in him. Everyone had this image of him, and suddenly he was painfully aware of the fact that it no longer fit. That, moreover, he didn't even like it anymore. That Ricky was acting *totally* out of character, and that the only way that could happen, barring outside interference, was if—

The realization struck him so hard that for a moment he couldn't breathe. "I'm out of here," he said, and headed for the door.

He almost ran to his quarters, his heart racing. Redemption. Here it was, finally. His chance to make everything right, to show everyone, especially her, that he wasn't so bad, that he could change, *had* changed.

*Her brown eyes, so soft and warm, were cold now. Her lips were pressed in a thin line, and her body was held aloof from his tender touch. So often, when she was like this, it had been easy to melt her with the right word, the touch in just the right spot.*

*"I can't handle it anymore," she said. "You keep promising that you'll change, and you don't. I don't think you even can, let alone want to. I've been with you for two and a half years now, and that's about two years and five months too long."*

*"Ricky . . ." he began.*

*"You know I don't like being called that. My name is Richenda."*

*"Of course it is, baby."*

*Now the cold eyes flashed. "I'm not your baby, damn it, Tom! I'm an adult and I have needs, and I do not deserve the way you treat me."*

The computer had found what he wanted. He leaned forward, listening eagerly, fearfully.

"Moriarty," it began in its cool, familiar female voice. "Professor James. A character created by Sir Arthur Conan Doyle in the Sherlock Holmes stories of the late nineteenth century. Designed as a holodeck program by Lieutenant Commander Data and refined by Chief Engineer Geordi La Forge aboard the starship *Enterprise. . . ."*

Harry smothered a grin at the satisfying click of the cue ball on the eight ball. The black ball rolled slowly toward the side pocket, seemed to consider its options, then dropped in obediently.

"I win again," he said to Gaunt Gary.

The holographic character frowned. "Maybe I ain't been so

nice to you, girl," he said to his cue, patting the shaft affectionately. "Get you a little more chalk next time."

Torres walked up to him. "Nice game. Can you be a little more obvious?"

"Hey, I like to win as much as the next guy," protested Kim. "Gary—rack 'em up, will you?" The simulation glowered at him. Harry turned to face Torres. "So, how do you think it's going?"

To his surprise, she looked troubled. "I'm not sure. Part of the fun was that he'd be here and we could watch what happened. The computer says he's been in his quarters, accessing the ship's database, for the last three hours. I'm going to go check on him."

"Don't blow it." He watched her go, her heels clicking against the simulated wood of Sandrine's floor, then looked over at the Doctor and Etta.

He grinned. The Doctor, who had only a few hours before been so infatuated with his clever etiquette program, looked utterly deflated. Etta looked exactly as she had looked when they first walked in. And she hadn't stopped talking. She had criticized how he placed his napkin, how he ordered dinner, how he spooned the soup, how he ate through three courses, and how he selected and sipped his after-dinner drink.

". . . and when a lady approaches, you should always rise," Etta droned on. "Your chair-holding needs work. Let's try it again."

"Etta, I'd rather not."

"You have been resisting my excellent advice all through the meal," she said. "One might think you didn't enjoy my company."

The Doctor gazed at her and stated bluntly, "I don't."

She gasped. "How extremely rude. We'll have to work on verbal courtesy next."

The Doctor smiled. "You know, I somehow don't think we will. Computer, delete etiquette program." Etta's eyes flew wide and she opened her mouth to protest.

"Permanently," he added.

Etta disappeared. The Doctor sighed, picked up the napkin

from his lap, crumpled it vigorously and then tucked it into his shirt at the neckline. "Garçon!" he called to one of the waiters. "A second dessert. Something gooey. And no utensils."

As the waiter hurried away, the Doctor smiled, gently and with tremendous satisfaction.

Kim chuckled.

*"You treat me like a, a pet, a plaything. I stayed because I love you, Tommy. My God, do I love you. I've taken treatment from you that I would never have stood for from anyone else, but it's over now."*

*"Fine with me, sweetheart," said Tom. "I don't care one way or the other. We had some fun, and—"*

*"Yeah, sure, we had some fun. A million laughs." She gazed at him with pity instead of anger in her dark brown eyes. "I know you don't love me, Tommy. And that's all right. What makes me feel so sorry for you is I'm not sure if you'll ever love anyone. And that's a frightening way to go through life."*

The door chimed softly. Paris jerked awake, realizing that he'd fallen asleep. Rubbing his eyes, he called, "Come in."

The door hissed open. Torres stood there for a moment, the soft lighting from the corridor playing over her features and casting them into a mosaic of shadow and light.

She sniffed. "Coffee? I thought you would be indulging in some exotic vintage, or a neat whiskey." She entered and regarded him evenly. "It's late. Aren't you going to go to bed?"

"Not right now."

"Are you planning on going to bed in the near future?"

"No."

"You ever going to bed?"

"No!" he shot back, starting to get annoyed.

"Then I'm not sleepy either." She sat down on the desk. "What are you working on that has you away from your own party drinking coffee alone in your quarters?"

His eyes searched hers; then he made a decision. "You might be able to help me out, at that," he said. He tapped in instructions to the computer. Instantly, a female face appeared on the screen.

"Do you know who this is?" he asked Torres.

She frowned. "It's your holographic sweetie, isn't it? Ricky? Though her hair's different and she looks a bit older."

Tom nodded. "It is . . . and it isn't. This woman is Richenda Masterson." She didn't seem to recognize the name. "The founder of the Interplanetary Art Exchange program."

B'Elanna chewed on her lip. "That sounds familiar—is she the one who takes groups of artists and visits different worlds? The one who invented the mathematical art theory?"

"Exactly. I knew her several years ago, when she was studying in France. We met at Sandrine's."

She looked at him with a new appreciation. "She's the only human artist I know of who's managed to impress both the Vulcans and the Klingons. You knew Richenda Masterson?"

Tom grimaced. "We were . . . involved, for a while."

Torres glanced away. "Oh. You don't have to tell me—"

"I know, but I want to. I need your help, and you've got to understand why. Richenda was one of the most amazingly talented and brilliant women I've ever met." He looked back at the screen, at the older but no less beautiful visage of "Ricky" Masterson. "I was the luckiest guy in the world. She loved me."

"What happened?"

"She left me because I treated her badly," Tom said bluntly. His voice was flat. "I wasn't in love with her and, damn me for a bastard, I played her like Harry plays that clarinet. The more hoops she jumped through for me, the less I thought of her—and the more hoops I held up. Finally, she had enough and walked out on me." His voice suddenly betrayed him, cracking a little. "Smartest thing she ever did."

Torres still wouldn't look at him. "Tom, there's something I have to tell you."

He ignored her. He was afraid if he stopped now, he'd never get it all out, and he had to tell Torres if he were to ever make it right.

"Back at the Academy, when I had girl trouble—she didn't notice me, or she wasn't nice, or whatever—I'd get my own sort of revenge. I'd start calling my ship by her name. That way, it was almost like being able to make the girl do whatever I wanted. Pretty childish, but I thought it didn't harm anyone. When Richenda left—I didn't want her to go. I wanted her to stay and be someone that I could handle. So from the minute I had my first opportunity to visit a holodeck and create my own programs, Ricky was in them. I made her do whatever I wanted her to do. She was always willing, always patient, she'd never leave me—"

"Tom, stop it!" Torres whirled on him suddenly. He couldn't read her expression, but she was agitated. "Harry and I—"

"It was wrong, and I know it was wrong. But I've got a chance to make it up to her!" Paris barreled on. "Don't you see? Something has happened with Ricky's program. She's not the same character I designed, and if nothing's gone wrong on the ship, then there's only one answer. Somehow, she's become sentient!"

"No, Tom—"

"It's happened before. Remember the Moriarty incident? We all got that lecture before going into the holodecks back at the Academy. I admit, the Moriarty program evolved because it was so complex, and Ricky was designed to be anything but, but it's happened and I need your help. If we can—"

*"Listen to me!"* Tom blinked, startled at her outburst. "It's not that, Tom. Ricky's not sentient. I—we—Harry and I decided to play a trick on you." She swallowed, hard, but kept her eyes locked with his. "I broke into your program and redesigned Ricky to make her behave more like a real person. I got so sick of her prancing around, and we thought it'd be funny. We had no idea about—that you'd take it so seriously. We thought you'd catch on right away, especially when Harry programmed your pool shark to lose all the time. I'm so sorry, Tom. It was just a joke."

He felt the blood drain from his face. Just a joke. He'd just bared his soul, dared to hope for a chance at correcting some of the obscenely cruel things he'd done when he was young and half-mad with pain and guilt over the accident back at the Academy, all because Kim and Torres thought it would be *funny* if—

"I hope you and Harry have a good laugh," he said, his voice eerily quiet. "Now get out."

"I've never seen him like that," Torres finished. Harry looked as miserable as she felt.

"I guess I can't blame him," said Harry softly.

A pool cue tapped on his shoulder. "How 'bout another round, kid?" asked Gaunt Gary.

"No, thanks." As the big pool shark strode away, his attention on Captain Janeway, who had also beaten him tonight, Harry added softly, "It's no fun anymore."

"You said it." Torres glanced about. It was very late. Nearly everyone else was gone, and Sandrine was starting to gather up the glasses. Neelix looked at the few crumbs that remained of the lavish feast and smiled. Captain Janeway declined an invitation to another game of pool and, on Chakotay's arm, headed for the door. The only other real people left in the holodeck were Harry and B'Elanna. Everyone else was a hologram, a figment of the imagination, and even they were going home for the "night." None of this was real. And yet, because of these illusions, she and Harry had inadvertently hurt their friend. Because of these illusions, Tom had done so much to hurt himself.

Harry yawned and rubbed at his eyes. "I'm going to turn in."

"You go ahead. I don't think he's going to show. We can catch him tomorrow and apologize."

He wandered through the heavy wooden doors and disappeared into the foggy night. Torres heard the doors to the holodeck hiss open, then shut.

She accepted the last glass of red wine and a neat scotch from

Neelix, who, sensing her troubled spirit, tactfully left her alone. Leaving the scotch untouched, Torres sipped the wine slowly.

She didn't like to lie, but she had lied to Harry just now. She did think Tom would show up one more time tonight. At least, she hoped he would. If he didn't, then he was more broken than even he knew.

Even the drunks had gone home, thought Paris as he opened the door to Chez Sandrine. The only reason the place was still open at this ungodly hour was because he had never bothered to program a closing time for the bistro. But there was a stillness about the place. Sandrine's might never close, but the characters did have set agendas.

Sandrine was there, of course, washing up. Yvette was performing her traditional final number, *"Non, je ne regrette rien."* The gigolo was in hushed, urgent conversation with his latest conquest. Gaunt Gary had put away his cue and was shrugging into his jacket. He gave Paris a curt nod, adjusted his fedora, and went out into the night.

And B'Elanna Torres was at the bar, nursing a final drink. She straightened, sensing his eyes on her, and turned around. Their eyes met for a long time. Then she smiled—a soft, sweet smile that he'd never seen from her before, that gentled her edgy Klingon features.

He liked that smile.

She put down her drink, thanked Sandrine, and picked up a shot glass of scotch. She glided past him without a word, pressing the scotch into his hand, and left the holodeck. He was, for all intents and purposes, given his privacy.

Now or never, Tommy, he thought, and closed his hand around the cool, small glass.

*"Non, je ne regrette rien,"* crooned Yvette. *I regret nothing.* An ironic anthem for Tom, who regretted nearly everything he'd ever done.

"Computer," he said. His voice cracked. "Computer," he repeated. "Activate holoprogram Ricky."

At once, she was there. She looked around, a bit startled; then her brown eyes narrowed as she saw him.

"You again."

He nodded. "Yeah. Listen, can we talk?"

"I don't—"

"Please." He could hear the pleading in his voice, but he didn't care. She just had to stay long enough to hear him out.

Ricky—Richenda—regarded him for a long, cool moment, then nodded. He gestured to the table by the fire, and they seated themselves. Sandrine glanced at them but declined to comment. Paris was grateful for that. For all her flirting, the real Sandrine was, at heart, a good woman, and he had programmed her doppleganger thus.

"I'd like to tell you a story," he began, running a finger idly over the rim of the shot glass. "It's a story about a young man who had a universe full of happiness, and was too much of a fool to realize it. This young man had friends, a family who loved him, and a promising career. But he was so busy thinking about what he didn't have that he got careless one day. And because of his carelessness, three people, his two closest friends and the woman he loved, were killed."

He didn't look at Ricky, but sensed her softening, her compassion. He kept his eyes on the table and continued.

"The young man was horrified. But he was also selfish. So he lied about the accident. But you know something? Lies aren't just words. Lies sit there in the pit of your stomach and eat you up from the inside out, until there's nothing left of you inside at all. You're just a walking shell, with darkness where your heart and guts should be."

Something warm brushed his back. Her hand, stroking, calming, wordless. That was how Ricky showed her sympathy—not with words, but gestures.

"So our empty young hero, with no heart and no guts left to speak of, tried to fill that emptiness with alcohol and women and parties. And the universe, which had always been so kind to him, one day gave him yet another kindness that he didn't deserve. It gave him a woman named Richenda Masterson, who had more talent and courage and intelligence in her little finger than he had in his whole rotten shell. But you know what? The young man was so eaten up inside he didn't realize what the universe had done. He hurt Richenda. He belittled her gift. He took from her and gave her nothing in return but contempt and disinterest, thus ensuring that the emptiness inside him would only continue to grow."

"That sounds like a sad story," said Richenda, her voice husky. "Does it have a sad ending, too?"

Now Tom looked at her. His heart almost broke. If only he could do it over again—

"I don't know. The last chapter hasn't been written." Hesitantly, he took her hand. He hadn't programmed the calluses into Ricky's hands. Richenda's work in stone and wood had made her fingers powerful and strong. She opted to keep the calluses and scars, though a dermal regenerator would easily get rid of them. She was proud of them, she told him; proud of what they symbolized. It was yet one more thing Tom had taken from Richenda.

"Do you understand that you're a hologram?" he asked her.

She nodded. "Of course."

"Let me tell you who you are. You are what I made of Richenda Masterson. When the real Richenda left me, I made you—Ricky. A Richenda who would never leave, would always wait for me, would never argue. I turned a wonderful, real human being into my own personal toy. When I saw you tonight, after B'Elanna had reprogrammed you—I wanted to make it up to Richenda."

There was no more anger in her face now, only sorrow and gentleness. She covered his hand with her own. "Tom—I'm just a hologram. I'm not Richenda."

He nodded. "I know. And I hope to God that someday I'll be able to tell the real Richenda just what I'm telling you. But I'm thousands of light-years from home, and I not only owe her an apology—I owe you one, too. I'm sorry."

Tears stood in her eyes. "I forgive you, Tom," she whispered. "And I think that, one day, Richenda will forgive you, too." She leaned forward and kissed him softly, without passion.

Tom savored the kiss, then pulled back. He stroked her face one last time, touched the thick softness of her dark hair. Lifting the scotch glass—the shot of courage B'Elanna had given him—he toasted her.

"Here's looking at you, kid." He downed the scotch and set the glass on the table. Only one more thing left to do, to make it as right as he could.

"Computer," he said, gazing into her eyes. "Delete hologram Ricky. Permanently."

She was still smiling as she disappeared.

Torres was waiting for him outside the holodeck entrance, leaning up against a bulkhead. They regarded one another for a long moment.

"How's Ricky?" she finally asked.

He took a deep breath, held it, exhaled. "Ricky won't be at Sandrine's anymore."

She ducked her head, not looking at him as she spoke. "I'm proud of you, Tom. That took courage."

Automatically Paris formed a flip comment, but the words died in his throat. He wasn't feeling flip, and the thought of faking his emotions right now suddenly made him slightly sick to his stomach. He tossed his coat over his shoulder, carrying it with his index finger. They walked in silence for a while.

"You know, honestly, I was getting kind of tired of Sandrine's, anyway," said Torres.

"Yeah, me too."

"How about another program? Like, maybe, pirates or something?"

He was suddenly very glad that she had waited for him. He glanced down at her and grinned. Pirates, huh?

"You know, B'Elanna," he said, "I think this is the beginning of a beautiful friendship."

# When Push Comes to Shove

## By Josepha Sherman and Susan Shwartz

Captain Janeway paused, glancing about *Voyager*'s bridge. All was calm: Tom Paris looked bored; Chakotay was lost in thought; and Tuvok was . . . Tuvok, which meant Vulcan-impassive. Harry Kim, at his station, was studying some onscreen calibrations with utter concentration—not surprising, since Seven of Nine was studying them over his shoulder and, presumably, making coldly analytical corrections.

Just another day on *Voyager*. Until . . .

"Captain!" Kim said sharply. "I'm picking up a distress signal . . . two-eight-zero mark thirty-five. One . . . ship, I guess," he added doubtfully. "It's, well, cobbled together, I'd say."

"A badly assimilated amalgam of parts," Seven agreed.

"On screen," Janeway ordered.

They all stared at the distressed ship in a moment of startled silence. Rusty, mismatched engines . . . gouges in one side patched with what looked like scrap metal. . . . Janeway's first thought was: *That can fly?* Her second was: *Not for much longer.* "Life signs?"

Kim was studying his console. "Six . . . no, seven life forms. Humanoid, oxygen-breathing, and—"

"Sensors indicate that life support is failing," Seven cut in. "The ship is venting atmosphere, and the structural integrity field has been compromised. It will collapse totally in four point three minutes." She added in cold disapproval, "Certifying what is obviously an almost derelict spacecraft as fit to fly is unproductive."

"We can discuss that later," Janeway said dryly. "Lieutenant Paris. Open a hailing frequency. *U.S.S. Voyager* to unknown vessel. Your distress signal is acknowledged. We are standing by to render assistance."

". . . thanks be . . ." came the weak reply, half lost amid static. "Please . . . child . . . at least save . . ."

The transmission ended in one final burst of static.

Janeway spoke into her combadge. "Captain to transporter room. Prepare for emergency transport from disabled ship. Seven persons. Sick Bay: Be ready to receive possible casualties. Mr. Neelix, meet me in the transporter room." Granted, *Voyager* was light-years away from "his" sector of space, but you never could tell what information Neelix might provide. Springing to her feet, Janeway added, "Chakotay, you have the conn. Tuvok, Seven, come with me." What Neelix didn't know, a Borg might.

*And never mind how she might have learned it,* Janeway added to herself.

The image of the damaged ship loomed over them on a remote monitor. Janeway glanced up at it, willing, *Hold on . . . hold on . . . we've almost got you. . . .*

Debris erupted from the derelict's nacelles. An instant later, Janeway winced as the ship blew apart in progressively brighter explosions and one final blinding glare.

"Did we get them?" she demanded.

Lieutenant Warren, a stocky, competent man, was at the console, his fair-skinned face red with concentration. "Signal's trying to break up . . . no, you don't . . . I'm reinforcing it . . . yes! Got them!"

Six . . . no, all seven figures were forming: The smallest, presumably the child, was clinging so tightly to an adult that it was almost hidden.

An adult *what,* though? The refugees were light-boned, almost birdlike in appearance, their narrow faces triangular, with high, prominent cheekbones beneath bright, dark eyes. They were also, understandably, disheveled and stained with ash, oil, and grime from their destroyed ship. Long, unruly crests of hair flowed down their backs in unruly tangles of blacks, browns, and bronzes, and their gauzy robes, almost as gaudy as Neelix's outfits and even more colorful under the stains, looked downright bedraggled.

*But they're all alive, and apparently unhurt.*

They were fully alert, too. Those bright glances flicked from Janeway to Tuvok to—

Ah, yes, here came Neelix now, hurrying into the room, shedding a chef's apron as he came. As he saw the new arrivals, he stopped dead with a laugh of sheer delight. "By the Great Tree, this is wonderful! Never would have expected to see any of you folks this far out of your range, but—just wonderful! Captain, our guests are none other than T'kari!"

"Yes," one of the refugees agreed in a clear tenor, smiling an almost human smile. "We are T'kari." He blinked. "Captain?"

Hearing her title, the T'kari surged forward, all of them delightedly chirping:

"Captain!"

"You are the one who spoke to us!"

"You saved us!"

"We are happy, grateful, yes!"

**114**

It was difficult to be alarmed by the fluttering lot, particularly since Janeway was a full head taller than any of them. And their near-hysteria was understandable: They'd just been snatched from death.

"Wait a minute," Janeway said, raising a hand. The T'kari obediently froze. "I am Captain Kathryn Janeway of the *U.S.S. Voyager*, and you are welcome on board. You are . . . Mr. Neelix called you T'kari. What and who are T'kari?"

Neelix's smile widened, and he almost danced with delight. "They're nomads, Captain, truly splendid musicians and entertainers who live on board their ships. Though, usually, the ships are in, well, better repair than that one was."

The T'kari who had first spoken, the tenor—a male?—said, "True enough, true enough. But that poor thing was the only refuge we could find. And yes, Captain Jane-e-way, we are performers."

Sure enough, he had a stringed instrument slung over his shoulder, while another T'kari had a small, long-stemmed drum. A lighter-boned . . . female? . . . carried a framework of tiny bells that tinkled faintly as she moved.

"And look," Neelix exclaimed, "that one, the elder"—he dipped his head in quick courtesy—"the elder actually has a Destiny Tarot."

The elder, a T'kari woman in filmy layers of red and violet robes, carried a battered deck of cards on which a gold symbol blazed.

Seven of Nine moved to Janeway's side. "Species 7509," she pronounced the newcomers. "Extreme manual dexterity and speed compensate for this species' relative physical frailty. They have vestigial telepathic abilities. We added their distinctiveness to our diversity and found ourselves even more efficient at micromanipulations."

Instead of the horror Janeway expected, the T'kari seemed . . . amazed.

115

"A pet Borg!"

"You have separated one out from the collective!"

"You have tamed a Borg!"

Genuine wonder? Or an oblique way of insulting Seven? Either way, she merely watched, expression unchanged. Janeway explained gently, "She is not a pet or a captive. Seven of Nine is a valuable member of our crew."

"Is it so? Is it so?" The elder's voice was deeper than Janeway had expected, a true alto. "Most amazing. But do not mistake what your valuable Borg says. We are not thieves!"

"We are the T'kari," the tenor added. "Which means, though we wander, we have honor. This is Inarra, and I am Andal."

The others added their introductions: Ekta, a soprano carrying a harp, Lirik, a baritone with what looked much like a lute, Eloan and Kalora, sopranos and pipers, all T'kari adults, though Eloan looked to be barely out of adolescence.

*Where's the child? There she is, still hiding behind them. Why haven't they introduced her? Custom? Or just giving the poor little thing a chance to catch her breath?*

"We are singers, sojourners, dwellers on the paths between the worlds," Andal continued. "We can repair what is broken. . . ."

"Apparently, Captain, this did not extend to their ship," Tuvok commented.

Inarra's bright, disapproving glance flicked to him. "A cook-unit, a zither with a snapped bridge, a ripped cloak: Those we can repair. A broken ship . . ." She gave an odd little twist of a shoulder: a T'kari shrug. "Such are in the hands of Destiny—which we can read, Captain, but which squirms away even from us at times."

"I see. And what," Janeway wondered aloud, "are we to do with you?"

"Three stars away," Andal said hopefully, "is the world Avanaram with its markets. You will surely find fresh supplies for your ship there. And if you take us there, we will be able to make a living, put a little away for another ship—one not so old as our lost *Eyrie*."

"Avan-aram?" Janeway asked Neelix, who shook his head. "I'm sorry, but you'll have to describe this world and its star system. Give us the coordinates if you can."

"We will try," Andal said uncertainly. The T'kari moved together, touching hands, eyes shut in sudden, intense concentration. Janeway blinked as an image of a planetary system formed in her mind: a yellow star, so like Earth's own sun that it was jarring to count only seven worlds about it. No, it was not home—but she suddenly knew how to get there.

And just as suddenly, the image was gone. The T'kari swayed and staggered, clinging to each other to keep from falling, clearly drained. "We have . . . only the faintest . . . of telepathic talents," Andal panted, clearly embarrassed. "Vestigial . . . yes. Once, stories say, our people had greater powers. Now . . ." He gave that twist of a shrug.

"Even vestigial telepathic powers may still be dangerous," Tuvok reminded Janeway.

*Not in this case,* she thought. *That was no feigned exhaustion. And so much work just to give me a star chart—no. They'd kill themselves before they could work any harm.* But she'd have the Doctor examine them thoroughly, just in case. "Neelix knows about these people, or thinks he does. Besides," she added with a quick little grin, "Neelix has been pestering us about fresh supplies."

Activating her combadge, she said, "Janeway to Sick Bay: Prepare to receive seven visitors." Cutting off the Doctor's predictable huff of outrage at being deprived of Tom Paris's services as nurse "while the man is playing pilot," Janeway contacted Paris next.

"Tom, lay in a course for Avan-aram on the following heading: 79X Mark 35. Warp factor two."

"*Aye, aye.*"

"We shall not trespass on your hospitality long," said Inarra with a sharp glance at Tuvok.

Andal nodded. "And while we're aboard, we shall offer our thanks by performing for you and your crew. Is that acceptable?"

Neelix was grinning so broadly and nodded so vehemently that Janeway nearly laughed. "It is highly acceptable. Seven, now you'll have a chance to hear some live music aside from Ensign Kim's clarinet—"

But Seven of Nine, her face utterly unreadable, had moved to study the child, who had come out of hiding to stare up at Seven. Was this truly another T'kari? Some genetic throwback to an earlier type, perhaps, or a child of a closely related species. It . . . she . . . was darker-skinned than the others, so light-boned that she seemed almost fragile. A long, tousled crest of black hair flowed over a crimson jacket and skirt that exposed bony wrists and ankles. Her triangular little face, with its huge dark eyes, was far too solemn for someone of her age . . . whatever that was. Ten, Janeway hazarded, at most.

And Seven, to Janeway's utter bemusement, sank to one knee to study the child more closely. For a long moment, neither moved, equally fascinated.

"Her name is Lari," Andal murmured to Janeway, his eyes gentle. "At least we think that's her name."

"We found the girl, lost and alone, crying with hunger in a marketplace," Inarra added. "She could tell us nothing of herself or her family, but she is clearly T'kari-kin. Besides . . . we could not leave the little one to starve."

"The entire troupe adopted her," Andal continued tenderly. "And we are raising her as best we can."

The child, Lari, brought up a wary hand to touch the implant on Seven's face.

Seven shied away, springing back to her feet. As though struggling to return to proper Borg coldness, she said to Janeway, "Al-

**118**

though the child seems to be of the same or a closely related species, Captain, the Collective has no additional knowledge."

*That was no Borg analysis you were making,* Janeway thought. *What just happened? Were you . . . remembering Annika?*

Neelix was kneeling beside the child now, murmuring something cheerful to her to make her smile. She gave the softest of giggles, but her gaze stayed on Seven.

*Poor little thing,* Janeway thought. *You've been through too much for a child so young.*

"The protective impulse you are all manifesting," Tuvok said in his most scholarly Vulcan tone, "is an example of neoteny, the attraction toward the very young, and part of a species' survival instinct."

But that observation, Janeway noticed, didn't stop him from moving to Neelix's side and holding up a hand to the child, his fingers parted in the Vulcan greeting. "Live long and prosper, Lari the Wanderer."

The child gave a tiny laugh of delight, trying to make her fingers match Tuvok's. She succeeded, and the Vulcan's dark face seemed to gentle.

"I'd say neoteny seems to be part of the Vulcan psyche too," Janeway noted. Did Tuvok see in this waif some echo of the family he had not seen for so long and the grandchild he had never met?

After one last smile at Tuvok, Lari returned to studying Seven—who was clearly growing disconcerted by the child's interest.

The Doctor was trying to contact Janeway. She activated her combadge in time to hear him snap, "Captain, I don't know what you're doing, but may I suggest that the best time to interrogate these people is *after* I have run them through Sick Bay? Perhaps you could have them sent here—and perhaps you could also *send Mr. Paris to help me!*"

"I'll take your request under advisement, Doctor," Janeway said carefully, refusing to laugh. "You are *Voyager*'s guests," she told the T'kari. "I'm sending you to Sick Bay—no, no, just to be sure none of you are injured. Regulations," she added, and saw the T'kari sigh in resignation. "You won't be harmed, my word on it. Tuvok, if you would see that they are properly escorted? And Mr. Neelix, please accompany them."

So far, so good. But as Janeway left the transporter room, Seven followed more slowly.

*What memories did that child spark in you?* Janeway wondered. *Can you be remembering Annika Hansen? Are you remembering being . . . merely a human child?*

She knew that if she asked, Seven would not respond. And, Janeway mused, it was just possible that Seven didn't know the answers, either.

Ah, well, back to the bridge. Sitting in her command chair, Janeway was about to add to that suddenly interrupted log when the Doctor sent her an acerbic message.

*"Our visitors are exactly what they seem: a group of frightened, weary humanoids, avian subgrouping 104.5A, no hazardous materials, no infectious diseases, nothing worse than a few minor contusions."*

"Have you tested for—"

*"Yes, Captain."* The Doctor sounded even more put-upon than usual. *"They do, indeed, have vestigial telepathic abilities, not enough to bend a spoon. Though why one should want to—"*

He was interrupted by a spurt of music. Very nice music, it seemed, too, Janeway thought. Flute and harp, was that?

*"There they go again! Captain, please, would you get these . . . these musicians out of Sick Bay and on stage where they belong?"*

Janeway grinned. "Gladly, Doctor. Gladly."

Seven of Nine, Tertiary Adjunct of Unimatrix Zero One, stood in her alcove. The vital flows of current restored her body, implants, and nanites, while the hum of the Collective rose about her.

In alcoves all around her rested similar drones, while others went about their appointed tasks, guided by the Collective and the song of the Borg Queen.

Resistance was futile. Resistance was superfluous.

That was the way of it. . . .

Or was it?

Loop. Restart.

Seven stood in her alcove in a cargo bay of *Voyager.* Physically ingested nutrients had restored her body; now, the current restored the eighteen percent of her that remained Borg. She no longer heard the song of the Collective, but the myriad sounds of a starship controlled by individuals as it traveled through deep space.

Her home had always been a ship, a ship populated by drones/a ship guided by a tall man, a laughing woman, with fair hair and blue eyes like her own/a ship commanded by a woman as formidable as the Borg Queen, who spoke to her and held out her hand.

*"Seven. Annika. Time to come out."*

Seven of Nine turned obediently, leaving the refuge of her alcove.

The T'kari waif called Lari was watching her. Confused for a moment at what was patent reality yet was at the same time impossible, Seven met the child's unblinking stare in what Ensign Kim called a glare, an expression one used when one wished to be left alone. "Cargo bay is no place for a child."

The "glare" failed to work.

"You were like me once," Lari said. "All alone like me."

"I had the Collective," Seven retorted. "You are merely alone." She suppressed the impulse to retreat into her alcove. Irrelevant. Nonfunctional.

"I hear the songs of my clan," the child countered.

"I will take you back to them. Now." She had learned that tone of finality from the Captain.

Seven felt the child's warm little hand unexpectedly close about her own, and nearly pulled free in shock. But . . . the child was lost . . . alone. . . . *I must return her to her adopted people.*

She came back to reality with a shock, wondering why she had not already asked the most important question. "How did you enter the cargo bay? I secured it before I entered my alcove. You would have needed to pass through several other secure areas as well. How?"

"I pushed," Lari said simply.

"That does not make sense. There is nothing to push."

"I pushed," Lari repeated.

The child sounded weary. For a bewildering moment, Seven felt an urge to pick the girl up and carry her—*the tall man cried "tired, Annika?" and swung her up, up, up to the sky before carrying her off to her bed with the bird-mobile over it. Ravens, just like their ship. . . .*

Ridiculous. She was Seven of Nine. She was Borg. She would return the child to her people, then consult with Captain Janeway.

They left the turbolift on Deck Six, where the T'kari had been lodged. But the turbolift doors had scarcely closed behind them when Seven saw one of the T'kari females—Eloan, the adolescent—hammering frantically on a door. "Inarra? Inarra! She's done it again!"

"Uh oh," whispered Lari. She tried to back away, but Seven tightened her grip on the girl's hand.

The door slid open, and Inarra's voice said tersely, "She will return soon. She always does. Return to your quarters, Eloan. They must not know."

*What? What must we not know?*

"Yes, Elder," the girl murmured.

The doors slid shut again.

*I must contact Captain Janeway.*

Turning to Lari, she said, "You will come with me, please."

The child wriggled her hand free and backed away, wide-eyed, around the bend of the corridor.

"I will not injure you," Seven said, wondering if the oddness she was feeling could possibly be . . . impatience, "but you must come with me."

Lari could not get very far. Seven followed the child around the curve of the corridor . . .

. . . and found no one there.

Janeway would be going off duty in . . . precisely seven minutes. Seven touched her combadge. "Captain, this is Seven of Nine."

*"Seven? What's wrong?"*

"Captain, I am on Deck Six. While there is no immediate peril, I have discovered . . . a matter here we must discuss. Please."

She made certain to use the verbal marker "please" so that the Captain would know that she did not attempt to usurp her command. There was a hint of a sigh from Janeway—who, being only human, had most probably been looking forward to going off duty. *"Very well, Seven. Meet me in my ready room."*

More racing footsteps—Eloan again, hammering on Inarra's door. "She's back!" Eloan's relief was evident, even to a Borg.

"Good." Inarra's voice was even more terse than before. "Now go back, quickly, before they find you running about like a summer-crazed *likta!* Try to sleep."

As Seven entered the ready room, she found a bemused and wary Janeway waiting.

"What is it, Seven?"

"I found the T'kari child near my alcove, which is a secure area, one for which, of course, she has not been authorized. She did not explain how she came to be there beyond saying that she 'pushed.' When I returned her to Deck Six, I overheard the other T'kari discussing her absence—and the need to conceal it from you. Almost immediately after that, the child . . . disappeared. I can only surmise that she 'pushed' again."

Janeway's raised brow meant, Seven knew by now, both annoyance and curiosity. "Thank you, Seven." Into her combadge she said, "Tuvok, have our T'kari visitors brought to my ready room, if you would."

*"At once, Captain."*

The Captain's smile, Seven thought, was not a friendly thing.

Janeway glanced about the ready room. Seven pairs of bright, alien eyes, as well as Seven's blue gaze, just as bright and almost as alien, stared back.

"People, I know you've been through a good deal of stress lately. And I know we're all weary. But I need some answers, and I need them now."

Andal glanced at the other T'kari. "Anything, Captain."

"Seven here says that she found Lari in a secure area. The child could not have gotten in there by any normal means. And before you suggest it," she added, seeing the glint in Andal's eyes, "none of my crew would have let her in there."

Janeway caught several quick, startled glances, birdlike little tilts of the head, T'kari to T'kari, but no one spoke. After a carefully timed pause, she continued, "And when Seven tried to return her to you, the child simply disappeared. Does that strike a chord with any of you? Yes? So, apparently, this isn't the first time that she's gone missing like this, either. Is it?"

Silence. Nervous glances.

*All right, go for the weakest member of the flock.* Janeway turned to the child, who flinched, staring up at her with wide, frightened eyes, "Lari, nobody's going to hurt you," she said. "But Seven says she saw you outside her alcove. When she asked how you got there, you said that you pushed. What did you mean by that?"

"Nothing. . . ." It was barely audible.

Janeway stifled a sigh. "No one's accusing you of anything bad, Lari. But a starship is no place for a little girl to run about unaccompanied. And if you're sleepwalking, the Doctor needs to know about it."

*Sleepwalking?* Janeway's mind echoed wryly. *Through solid walls?*

*Enough.*

"Lari, all of you," Janeway snapped. "You owe me your lives. And I'm calling in the debt right now. If you wish us to take you to Avan-aram, I need a full explanation. Now."

Sighs. Shrugs. Then Inarra began tentatively, "We mean you and your ship no harm, our honor on it."

"Go on."

Inarra glanced at Andal. He continued, "Your crewmember has called us vestigial telepaths. You have seen the truth of that. And you have heard me say that once we were more than we are now."

He paused, and Inarra took up the story again. "We found Lari alone as we said, and took her in. Among the T'kari, all are family. But we soon realized that she is of an older blood than we. And in her, some of the . . . ancient gift still runs strong."

"You don't seem precisely thrilled about that," Janeway said.

The T'kari glanced at each other yet again, more of those quick little birdlike movements. Inarra laughed softly. "It is not a gift without a sharp edge, a . . ." She held up a helpless hand.

"Mixed blessings?" Janeway suggested.

"Yes! Indeed! Most poetic phrasing. A 'mixed blessing.' T'kari gifts illumine our lives, but they are, truly, a 'mixed blessing,' since they also sometimes cause people to fear us, to turn on us or even seek to enslave us. When the gift is very strong, as Lari's is, it becomes a threat and a lure. My grandchild-of-the-heart does not read hearts and minds, but she has the power to move . . . to move herself."

"Teleportation?" Janeway exclaimed. "A natural teleporter?"

"Indeed, that. When we first adopted her, the gift was weak, only enough to let her evade us when she did not wish her face washed. Now, though, as she is growing stronger . . ."

Lari had "pushed" from Deck Six to Seven's alcove, Janeway thought. An older Lari, fully grown, fully trained . . .

The lights in the ready room suddenly flashed red/off, red/off, and the warning siren shrilled. *Oh, hell,* Janeway thought, and hit her combadge. "Chakotay! What's going on?"

*"We've been hailed by a ship of a sort I've never seen before. They want to talk with the captain. And they've brought their weapons online."*

"On my way. Janeway out." She leaped to her feet, a hand stabbing at Andal and Inarra. "You two, come with me. And you, too, Seven. The rest of you, stay here!"

A quick call to Security ensured that they would obey.

As Janeway stepped onto the bridge, she glanced at the viewscreen. Oh, yes, the ship hanging there in space was undeniably built for war. Ugly as the proverbial sin, it bristled with gunports. It had seen hard use, and probably could have taken something as small as the T'kari ship with no trouble at all. But something as large and powerful as *Voyager* . . . well now, that would be another matter.

*Don't underestimate them,* Janeway warned herself.

Chakotay rose, relinquishing the command chair.

"As far as I can tell from what little they would admit to someone who wasn't the captain, they call themselves Morak."

"Species 7611," Seven cut in coldly. "A warrior race of rigid determination but little imaginative scope. We added their unyielding strength to our diversity."

"Ah . . . thank you, Seven," Chakotay said. "Their ship emerged from"—he gestured at the screen—"that asteroid belt, between us and Avan-aram."

Janeway bit back a sigh. "And let me guess: They're not here to discuss anything as simple as right-of-way."

Chakotay gave her a wry grin. "I couldn't tell you what they want, since they refuse to talk to—"

"Anyone but the captain. Very well, let's see what they have to say. Open a hailing frequency," she ordered. As an image formed on the viewscreen, Janeway said, "To the Morak ship: You wished to speak to the captain? Well . . . here I am. I am Kathryn Janeway, captain of *U.S.S. Voyager.*"

The image resolved into a bridge much smaller and shabbier than *Voyager*'s, and focused on three humanoid figures seated in worn, uncomfortable-looking chairs. They wore dulled metal helmets, bulky sidearms, and uniforms of a drab gray-green that Janeway thought looked as old and uncomfortable as the chairs. The image was sharp enough to let her see where harness and military insignia had been fastened over painstaking repairs.

*Not quite as well equipped as we'd like to be, are we?* That didn't mean they wouldn't be fierce or possibly even irrational, judging from what Seven had said about "little imaginative scope."

"Do you fear to show your faces like honorable warriors?" Janeway challenged.

The Morak in the center seat raised pale, seven-fingered hands to remove its—no, his—helmet, revealing an equally pallid face, thin-lipped, with a nose that was little more than a narrow ridge between slit-pupiled indigo eyes.

"*Voyager*-Captain." He dipped his head in what Janeway assumed was captain-to-captain courtesy. "What do you in this system?"

"We're on our way home," Janeway replied. "After dropping off some friends in a safe place."

"Ahhhh." It was as much a hiss as a sigh. "You have a fine ship. It would be sinful to destroy it."

"I am gratified to hear that," Janeway said dryly. "I assure you, we have no quarrel with the Morak, nor will we be stopping in this system for longer than it takes to drop off our friends. Will you let us pass?"

"Regrettably, *Voyager*-Captain, I cannot. Your ship carries T'kari. They are a shiftless, impious lot. But . . . we have uses for them."

"The T'kari are our guests," Janeway countered.

"Ahhhh, is it so? I will come to an agreement with you, *Voyager*-Captain. The Morak are not unreasonable. If you have a use for jugglers and petty thieves, very well, keep them. But they have with them a child, an innocent who must not be allowed to be tainted by impiety. Give her to us, and leave in peace. Fail," he added without the slightest change in tone or expression, "and we will blow you out of space."

"We will . . . consider it. End transmission."

As the screen went dark, Janeway turned to glare at Andal and Inarra. "Why are the Morak after you?"

Andal winced. "The Morak have a . . . rigid society. They consider our wanderings from world to world as improper, our songs and stories as sacrilegious. Above all, they distrust our gifts."

"That little exchange I just had with the Morak was about more than distrust. Am I correct in suspecting they know what Lari can do?"

The T'kari exchanged quick, sharp glances. "Unfortunately, yes," Andal admitted reluctantly. "A Morak spy saw her once, when she wasn't being careful, and reported to his superiors. All of a sudden, our poor powers became 'military assets.' The Morak tried to—to *buy* Lari from us, and when we refused—"

Inarra laid a calming hand on the man's arm. "Captain, this one Morak vessel has been tracking us from world to world. We fought to escape. We even drove our poor ship to destruction in the effort! We . . . dared think that we finally *had* escaped. But now . . ." She gave a sad little shrug.

"And this is the whole truth?" Janeway asked, staring into Inarra's eyes. "There aren't going to be any more surprises?"

Inarra met her stare steadily, despair plain on her face. "None. Captain, understand: We feared. We did not know you or your kind. Yes, you rescued us. But we did not know if, once you learned of Lari's gift and the pursuit—we did not know if you would not simply toss us into space." She sagged wearily. "Do as you must. Only . . . they must not harm Lari."

*I'm willing to bet that this time every word was open truth. And damned if I'm going to surrender a child to anyone who throws words like "impiety" about so casually!*

Janeway turned back to the viewscreen. "Open a hailing frequency. To the Morak ship: Hear my decision. The T'kari are under our protection. We will not betray them."

"*Voyager*-Captain, I am disappointed at such impiety. One last chance: Hand over that child to us, and we shall not bar your way. Else, we shall regret your deaths."

"*No!*" With a rush of displaced air, Lari was there on the bridge, staring at the viewscreen in horror. She darted toward the turbolift, then turned at bay, as if realizing that she could hide nowhere on *Voyager* without jeopardizing it.

"You're Captain Arwaig—I know you are!" she screamed at the viewscreen. "I saw what you did on Gwaran Three. But I won't let you hurt my family, my—my friends! I won't, I won't, *I won't!*"

With a new rush of air, Lari disappeared.

Janeway hastily broke off communications with the Morak. "Ensign Kim?"

"I think . . . yes! I've got a fix on Lari's vital signs. Apparently, she pushed onto the moon of the fourth planet out, the big one just beyond the asteroid belt. Lucky for her, it has decent gravity and atmosphere."

Inarra pressed her palms together. "She has never pushed that far, Captain. Is she well?"

"Life signs are strong," Kim answered. "But there's a lot of seismic activity on that moon."

"I must deplore attributing Lari's choice of habitable world to 'luck,' Ensign Kim," Tuvok said. "I would hypothesize that the child's ability to teleport herself must be, of necessity, linked to her instinct for survival. The child 'sees' that she will arrive in an environment capable of sustaining life."

"The Morak ship has begun to move toward the planet's satellite," Seven's voice cut in.

*Damnation.* "Tuvok! We'll move to a high orbit around the moon and beam a rescue team down to locate Lari before the Morak can find her. Take—"

"Me!" Andal pleaded, and Janeway nodded. A familiar face would be important for Lari to see.

"Captain," Seven cut in, "I must be included as well."

Empathy for a lost little girl? Or merely Borg policy, to leave no drone unrescued as long as rescue was possible?

"Consider yourself volunteered, Seven. Report to the transporter room."

*Unfortunate,* Seven thought as the transporter effect dissipated from about the rescue party and they saw their surroundings. This was a world of looming cliffs and narrow canyons striated in black, bronze, and rose and glittering with bits of crystal. The cliff walls were pitted by countless holes suggesting a network of caves and tunnels. The complex geology would make finding the child that much more difficult.

*However, it will also make it that much more difficult for the Morak to land a shuttle.*

The seismic instability Seven's instruments had detected were, to her Collective-trained mind, a greater hazard than the Morak. After all, one could neither kill nor assimilate a quake.

Ensign Kelvan, studying her instruments frantically, complained, "Static! All those crystals . . ."

"Keep searching," Tuvok told her.

The ground shook, sending pebbles rattling down the sharp slopes, then abruptly stilled.

"Prudence," Tuvok said with Vulcan calm, "would dictate standing away from the cliffs."

Another tremor shook the ground, stronger this time. A boulder came crashing down, showering them all with rock splinters.

Andal groaned. "It feels as though this moon is building up for a big quake. If Lari's hiding in one of those caves . . ."

The anguish in his voice . . . *"Get underneath the desk, Annika, hide," said the tall man. "I won't let them hurt you."* Seven blocked the unwelcome flash of memory. "Lari's ability to teleport will enable her to escape."

"Not if she's hit on the head, or—"

"Commander!" Ensign Kelvan said suddenly. "I'm showing life signs at zero-three-fifty mark five. Over there!"

"Lari!" Andal gasped, and started forward. Seven tackled him, and they both crashed to the ground—as an energy beam sizzled by where they'd been a moment before: too near a miss.

"That was not Lari," Tuvok said laconically as the team dove for cover.

"The Morak!" Andal cried. "If they have her . . ."

"They would have no need to shoot at us," Seven finished.

"We don't know that! Let me go!"

Light-boned though he was, Andal was frantic enough to tear free and run—only to cry out as a second beam struck him. As he crumpled, Seven, bent double to avoid presenting a target, raced after him.

"Get him into cover!" Tuvok shouted at her. She saw the rock he was pointing at, shouldered Andal, and ran for it.

"A flash burn," she called to Tuvok after a quick examination of the T'kari. "Not fatal."

The chief risk would be shock, so Seven pulled off her jacket and wrapped it around the half-conscious Andal to keep him warm, trying not to jolt his wound.

Could he hear her? Not certain why she should feel it necessary, Seven told him, "We will bring her home." Then, she remembered the magic words, the ones her father had almost never used, but meant every time he said them. "I promise," she added.

Seven touched her combadge, about to order that Andal be beamed up to Sick Bay—

She heard nothing but static.

\* \* \*

"Trouble, Captain," Tom Paris said suddenly. "The Morak are opening their gunports."

*They can't possibly believe they can take us.* But Seven had also said something about "rigid determination." *Translate that as "pigheadedness,"* Janeway thought. But that didn't mean the Morak might not do some damage. And with an away team on that moon, it was a risk she couldn't afford to take.

"Red alert," Janeway ordered. "Shields up. Open a hailing frequency," she added. "Let's see if we can't keep them talking . . . ah, yes. Captain Janeway to Morak captain . . . Arwaig, is it?" No answer. "Janeway to Morak captain: I know you're receiving. I also know that for you to fire on *Voyager* would be a bad mistake on your part." No answer. "Come now, Captain, think about this. Let us talk about the relative size and strength of our ships, shall we?"

"They're firing!" Paris cut in.

"I'll take that as a 'no.' "

*Voyager* rocked slightly as a bolt of orange energy dissipated against its deflector shields.

"Shields holding, Captain."

"No damage, Captain."

*Wonderful, just wonderful. The Morak look like uninspired fighters, but stubborn enough. Still, we can take anything that ship throws at us. We're safe enough—unless this Captain Arwaig calls in reinforcements. We could blow him out of space, but I'm not about to commit murder, or risk my own people.*

*I already have enough of my own people at risk. While we have shields raised, our away team is trapped down there—alone with the Morak.*

Tuvok listened intently to the message crackling from his combadge, then said, "I could not receive a clear signal. But it would seem that the Morak have begun firing upon *Voyager.*"

Andal stirred weakly. "It's our fault," he moaned. "Your poor ship . . . and how many of your people have those murdering thieves killed?"

"I assure you, *Voyager* finds the Morak less intimidating than you do. And," Tuvok added, looking about sharply, "less formidable than we will find an armed landing party. The ship will have raised deflector shields, and until it can safely lower them, we cannot expect to return."

"Then we must act on our own," Seven said.

She slipped around the base of the rock toward Ensign Kelvan's shelter, checking the tricorder reading against the cliffs, which were pockmarked by caves. Third cliff to the left, two levels up— or the mountainside equivalent thereof—*almost like a hive of the Collective,* Seven thought. Challenging enough for a frightened child to climb and consider herself safe: Simple enough for Seven to follow. Simpler still if she need not concern herself with quakes and Morak fire.

Something stirred within the cave and moved forward. Seven saw a flash of red. Lari!

"She is attempting to climb down."

A blaze of blue-white fire struck the cliff. Seven looked away, her Borg vision recalibrating itself. To her bewilderment, her heart was racing. When she looked back, the impact zone glittered, fused to glass by the Morak energy beams.

"Lari . . . ?" Seven searched the cliff. "There! She is crouching in the mouth of the cave."

"Apparently," Tuvok observed, "the Morak have decided that if they cannot have Lari, no one can."

"Unacceptable," Seven snapped.

There was no point in asking permission of Tuvok that he would not grant. She had been wise to shed the cumbersome jacket. She could run much more efficiently without it.

Behind her, Seven heard Tuvok shout, "Keep firing! Cover her!" She lunged forward, crouching, darting from rock to rock, then hurled herself at the cliff face. Finding footholds and handholds by touch and fierce will, Seven forced herself up and up again, Morak fire blazing and crackling about her. Suddenly her hands were closing about the lip of the cave, and she pulled herself inside, pouncing on Lari and pushing the girl away from the cave's mouth.

Nothing happened, other than Lari's inexplicably choosing to throw both arms about her and cling. Inexplicable, yet . . . not unpleasant.

For now, Seven decided, they were safe.

Then the ground shook, and she revised her opinion. Rocks crashed down from the roof of the cave, and Seven hunched over Lari to protect her, grunting at the impact as she was pelted with stones. The tremor ended, and she straightened, doing a quick self-examination.

"Are you all right?" Lari's voice was shrill with fright.

"Yes. Contusions and scrapes, no serious damage. But it is only a matter of time," Seven said, "until this cave becomes more dangerous than the Morak."

"But you shouldn't be here! It's my fault they want to hurt you!"

"If we remain here, the issue of blame will become irrelevant. Lari, can you push us back to Commander Tuvok? Or push yourself back to the ship?" Once the child was out of danger, *Voyager*'s crew could efficiently defeat the Morak.

Lari squeezed her eyes shut until her face contorted.

"I'm sorry, I'm sorry, you're too big! And there's a . . . a wall blocking me from the ship."

The child's talents clearly did not yet extend to more than her own body mass. And clearly, they were impeded by *Voyager*'s deflector shields.

The ground trembled again, and a crystal crashed down from the cave's ceiling like a glass knife, sending sharp slivers flying.

But . . . a crystal. . . . A sudden surge of Borg knowledge told her that crystals were natural resonators. Did immense crystals like these have immense natural resonating capacity to match? Quickly, Seven activated her tricorder, scanning with Borg swiftness. . . .

"They're coming!" That was Tuvok's voice, echoing up among the cliffs.

*The resonance should be strong enough. Barely.*

"Come, back in here, Lari. Where the crystals are most densely concentrated."

"They'll break! They'll cut us!"

"We must take the risk. I need you to push now, as hard as you can. Push for both of us. The crystals will focus and intensify your strength, and let you break through the wall you felt."

Seven heard scrabbling one cave-level below them: The Morak were climbing.

"Hold fast to me," Seven ordered. "Very well now. *Push!*"

The ground shook beneath them. "I can't!" Lari wailed.

"You can," Seven insisted. "Fear is irrelevant. *Push!*"

"You don't understand! You don't understand anything!"

"Do you want the Morak to catch us?"

"No! *No-o-o-o!*"

The cave shook. All about her, crystals snapped and shattered, a world of shining, dazzling light—

—nothing—

And then there was . . . *Voyager.*

The gleaming walls of *Voyager*'s bridge surrounded them. All around them, people were crying out in astonishment.

Beside Seven, Lari struggled to her feet, staggering. But then the child froze, face white with horror and exhaustion, staring at the Morak ship on the viewscreen, staring at the energy blazing from its weapons. "No, no, no!" she screamed at the Morak. "I don't want any more of this. Go home! Just—*go home!*"

The Morak ship shot away as though at top warp speed, almost instantly shrinking to a dot on the viewscreen.

"What the hell . . ." Paris breathed.

"Captain . . ." Kim stopped, then tried again. "I don't know how she did it, but . . . the Morak are out of range. *Well* out of range."

With the softest of sighs, Lari collapsed.

"Doctor to the bridge," ordered Janeway. "Stand down from red alert. Transporter room: Four to beam up."

The Doctor shook his head, his most disapproving frown on his face. "Captain, I really must protest the way everyone in this Sick Bay seems determined to suffocate my young patient."

"Sorry, Doctor."

Janeway took a step back and bumped into Seven of Nine, who had dismissed suggestions that she might need to regenerate in her alcove. Seated on a biobed, favoring his shoulder, was Andal, watching his adopted daughter's face as she slept. Elder Inarra shuffled her Destiny Tarot from hand to hand, while the other T'kari crowded in behind her.

Relenting ever so slightly, the Doctor added, "Children of all species are amazingly resilient. Lari just needed to have her sleep. But now that we're in orbit around Avan-aram, I suppose no harm will be done if I wake her."

Janeway heard the hiss of a restorative, then the whimper of a child awakened too early.

"It's all right, Lari," she soothed. "You're among friends."

"Among family," Elder Inarra said firmly.

Lari looked warily about, sat up, then hurled herself from the bed like a small meteor, hugging Janeway, Andal, Inarra, even the stunned Seven.

Inarra sighed. "I suppose every family has a member who is both valuable and a menace."

"Your fears are baseless," Seven said. "Lari will assimilate her gift properly with time."

*Will she?* Janeway wondered, and moved to Lari's side, kneeling beside her. "Lari, we need to talk about something."

"My . . . my gift."

"Exactly. It isn't always easy growing up, and it isn't always easy to remember to do the right thing. But you can do something most people can't. You'll always have to think before you use it, and be careful to use it only to help people."

Lari winced. "I . . . I know. I was mad enough to push the Morak ship into the sun. But I . . . well . . . I could hear them before I pushed. They were *scared*. I—I couldn't hurt them after that." She paused. "Do you hear them being scared when you fire the ship's weapons?"

Janeway looked into the child's eyes. They were much too wise for such a little girl.

"Every time," she said. "Every time." She took a deep breath. "Keep thinking like that, and you're definitely on the right track."

Janeway got to her feet. "Now, everyone," she said, "Elder Inarra says that you're all going to sing for us. I, for one, have been looking forward to this!"

Janeway and Seven stood on the observation deck watching the Avan-aram system recede.

Janeway grinned. "You enjoyed the performance, didn't you, Seven?"

"The level of energy expenditure focused solely on entertainment is irrational."

"Really? Then why did I catch you tapping your foot in time with the drumbeat?"

"The rhythmic patterns intrigued me," Seven replied with frosty dignity. But then, to Janeway's surprise, Seven added, "Will the T'kari be safe?"

"I think so. Inarra told me that Avan-aram values entertainers and likes the T'kari. They'll be able to earn a new ship and keep on traveling—away from the Morak, of course.

"Now, I'm going to tell Master Leonardo about the T'kari. Care to join me?"

She turned toward the corridor, then paused. Seven was still gazing downward, her expression unreadable. With a silent sigh, Janeway returned to her side. "No, Seven, nothing's ever neat and simple in life. But . . . maybe one day Lari will come and find us. She'll be older and stronger then.

"Who knows? Maybe she'll even be strong enough to give us a push . . . all the way home."

# The Space Vortex of Doom

## By D. W. "Prof" Smith

Captain Proton fought the controls of his spaceship like a cowboy trying to control a bucking horse—hard at times, then gently, then hard again as needed. The levers moved under his sure hands: back and forth, back and forth.

But the ship seemed to have a mind all its own, fighting him, slowing as if it were caught in thick mud.

"Turn on the Imagizer!" he ordered.

A gray vision filled the panel in front of him. The grayness seemed to be alive, swarming, surrounding the ship.

Constance Goodheart screamed!

"We're doomed!" Buster Kincaid exploded.

The Imagizer in front of Captain Proton showed nothing but a gray fog, thicker than any soup. No sign of open space at all.

But Captain Proton knew this was no fog. "Minions!" he exclaimed, fighting even harder at the controls, trying to force the ship by sheer will through the mass that surrounded them.

Push!

Shove!

Yank!

His hands worked the spaceship's controls.

Nothing!

No instant response like he normally got from his ship. No banking turns, no feeling of thrust into the ether.

"It's not working!" Buster Kincaid shouted. "They've stopped us cold in space!"

"Keep the engines on full speed ahead!" Proton ordered his trusty friend and ace reporter. "We'll make them work to keep us here."

"Engines on full!" Kincaid said. "Still not moving!"

Captain Proton knew why, too. Standing at the control panel, he braced himself and kept his hands firmly on the controls, hoping for a slight opening in the gray, squirming fog that covered the Imagizer in front of him—anything at all that might give them a chance to escape from the dreaded cloud of Minions.

Each Minion was an ant-sized flying creature with a smooth forehead and almost no brains. But the Minions had the ability to work together through telepathic means. And the ability to fly in space. Individually, they were nothing more than annoying bugs. But working together, in clouds of billions, they could stop a spaceship dead in the void, just as they had just done to his ship.

Within an hour, they would crush the ship. As far as Captain Proton knew, no one had ever escaped a cloud of Minions. Despite their tiny size, they were the most feared creatures of the spaceways. Normally they kept to their own system—but now they were a long way from home, surrounding his ship. Captain Proton didn't like that idea at all. It meant something had changed about them, or someone was controlling them.

Suddenly the Imagizer flickered, and the gray fog of Minions was replaced by the devilish face of Dr. Chaotica, the meanest man in all of known space. Chaotica's stated goal was to control the entire Galaxy, and he would use any means to do so. The only things that stood between him and Galaxywide domination was Earth, the Incorporated Planets, and the Interstellar Patrol, of which Captain Proton was a member.

Captain Proton knew immediately who was controlling the Minions.

Dr. Chaotica laughed—a long, evil sound that made Captain Proton's blood run cold.

Constance screamed again.

"What do you want, Chaotica?" Proton demanded, taking his hands from the controls and placing them on his hips in a show of defiance.

"It seems I have what I want," Chaotica said with a wicked laugh. "You are trapped by my Minions. You will soon be crushed. And to make my day perfect, my Blaster Ship is finished." Again his laugh filled Captain Proton's ship, leaving its evil touch on every surface, every dial, every button, like a film of scum.

Captain Proton could feel the blood in his face draining away. The Blaster Ship that Chaotica referred to was the only one in all the Galaxy. It was huge and powerful. The rumors said it was powerful enough to move entire suns. Proton knew that Chaotica's Blaster Ship, if it was finished, would be death to Earth and the Patrol. His mission had been to make sure it was never finished.

Chaotica had just told him he was too late.

Captain Proton forced himself to stare back at Chaotica. "I'd say there is still some time left in this day," Proton said defiantly. "We shall see who smiles at the end of it all!"

"The pleasure of watching you die would be all mine," Chaotica chortled. "But I'm afraid I don't have time for such small details. Earth awaits me!"

Then he broke the connection, leaving the three valiant heroes in silence in their doomed ship.

"What are we going to do?" Kincaid wondered.

"First," Proton answered, "we're going to get out of this cloud of Minions. Chaotica might be able to control them, but his Minions can't hold us!"

"How?" Kincaid asked, clearly surprised.

Proton smiled at his best friend. "Just do as I say, and watch," he said, again grasping the control levers of his Patrol ship. "Constance, grab something and hold on tight."

The blonde secretary nodded, grabbing a nearby railing while staring at the gray mass of Minions on the Imagizer.

"Are the engines still on full forward?" Proton asked.

"They are," Kincaid replied.

"Good. On my command, throw them into full reverse."

"That might blow everything up!" Kincaid cried, a worried look on his face.

"I know my ship," Proton said reassuringly, his hands grasping the controls. "Just do it. Now!"

Kincaid flipped the switch, sending the ship's engines into full reverse—a mode rarely used in space.

Everything bumped and vibrated around them, as if a giant hand was trying to shake the ship apart. But Captain Proton could feel the ship move. The Minions' grip on them clearly wasn't as tight as Chaotica had thought.

Captain Proton waited until the backward movement of the ship slowed, then shouted, "Now full forward!"

Kincaid did as he was told, flipping the switch back to forward thrust.

Smoke drifted from two panels.

Sparks flew everywhere.

Constance screamed!

A drop of sweat formed on Captain Proton's forehead, but he ignored it, instead focusing on the feel of the ship as it rocked back, then forward in the mass of Minions. This time the ship moved a little farther, a little quicker.

He waited as the motion slowed.

Waited.

Waited. . . .

Then at just the right moment he shouted, "Now reverse again!"

Kincaid did as he was ordered, flipping the switch back.

It was as if the ship had run head-on into a giant moon. Everything shook.

Sparks flew.

Smoke filled the room.

But Captain Proton could tell his idea was working. He was treating the ship as if it were an automobile stuck in the snow. The Minions were strong enough to hold the ship from moving in one direction, but not both. He could rock his way back and forth and get out.

This time they were moving backward at a good speed. Almost free.

He waited again until the Minions outside slowed the ship nearly to a stop, then shouted, "Now, Kincaid! Full power forward! Give it all you've got!"

Buster flipped the switch again, throwing the ship into forward, then twisted the dial that increased the thrust to maximum redline power. The ship had nothing left to give.

Everything shook.

Sparks flew!

Smoke poured out of every opening!

Constance screamed!

"Don't worry, my dear!" Proton said, shouting to make himself heard over the roar of the engines and the shaking of the entire ship.

He grasped the controls firmly, shoving the pointed nose of the ship directly forward through the Minions like a needle through skin.

The ship bucked.

Kincaid was tossed away from his station and smashed into a panel.

"You all right?" Proton shouted over the intense noise.

"Fine!" Kincaid returned as he scrambled to his feet.

Captain Proton kept his steely gaze focused dead ahead. This was their only chance. The ship wouldn't hold together for another try at full power.

He could tell they were breaking loose.

They were gaining speed!

Suddenly the Imagizer showed clear space in front of them.

Captain Proton cut the ship low into the gravity well of a nearby moon, using it to slingshot them into the depths of space and away from the cloud of Minions.

"We're free!" Kincaid rejoiced.

Constance beamed.

But Captain Proton remained firm at the controls, his face stern, his look frozen straight ahead. "Earth is in great danger. We must stop Chaotica and his Blaster Ship!"

"But how?" Kincaid asked. "Not even the entire Patrol can stop a Blaster Ship."

"Maybe the entire Patrol can't . . ." Proton replied, "but maybe one man can!" He stared ahead at the emptiness of space as he sped after Chaotica and his Blaster Ship.

"You have a plan!" Kincaid beamed.

"I have a plan," Proton answered. "Full speed ahead!"

Soon the giant bulk of Chaotica's Blaster Ship filled the Imagizer. It was long and sleek-looking, sort of like a giant silver bullet, the biggest thing Proton had ever seen—a hundred times bigger than the ship they were on.

It had a sharp, needle-nose front and six large fins along the back half, which kept it stable. On each of the six fins, a massive jet shoved the Blaster Ship through the ether. Clearly, Chaotica was heading for Earth at full speed. Luckily, Captain Proton's ship was faster.

Giant weapons stuck out from the nose of the Blaster Ship—weapons that could destroy an entire planet at the flick of a single switch. The Blaster Ship couldn't be allowed to get anywhere near Earth!

"We're going to sneak up behind him," Captain Proton observed.

"Brilliant!" Kincaid chortled. "Chaotica thinks the Minions have destroyed us, so he won't be looking for us."

"Exactly! Take over the controls, Kincaid," Proton ordered. "Fly us right between the huge jets."

Kincaid suddenly broke into a massive sweat as he took the controls of the ship. "Between the jets? We'll be killed!"

Proton patted his trusted friend on the back. "There's enough room, and you're a good pilot," Proton reassured him. "Just get us in there so I can jump to the service hatch."

"You're going inside?" Kincaid shouted, glancing back at where Captain Proton was putting on his space gear.

"Yes," Proton answered as he quickly finished donning his vacuum suit. "It's the only way to stop the ship." He moved toward his ship's airlock. "Now fly us between those jets to that service hatch."

Kincaid nodded. Carefully he inched the sleek, silver craft of Captain Proton between the fins of the giant ship. A few seconds later he bumped the nose of Proton's ship lightly against the service hatch of Dr. Chaotica's massive Blaster Ship and let out a huge sigh.

"Well done!" Proton exclaimed.

Around them the rockets of Chaotica's ship sent great plumes of fire into space, heating up the insides of Proton's ship like a toaster.

Captain Proton saluted his good friend Kincaid, then kissed Constance on the cheek.

"Good luck," said his faithful secretary. "Please be careful."

"Don't worry, my dear," Proton said, donning his helmet. Then, to both of his companions, he added, "It's going to get hot in here while I'm gone. But stay and wait for me. I will return!"

"Understood," Kincaid replied, saluting back. "No matter how hot it gets, we'll be here."

Proton nodded, then quickly went through the hatch into space. It didn't take him long to get inside the dark regions of Dr. Chaotica's Blaster Ship. The ship was simple in design, so he easily figured out how to get where he wanted to go. . . .

In the control room of the massive ship, Dr. Chaotica stood, staring through his Imagizer at the space ahead. There were only two other men in the room—one flying the ship, and one manning the weapons panel, ready to fire on any vessel that dared to try to stop them. But no ship would dare. The Blaster Ship was too large, too powerful.

Captain Proton came in silently, his gun drawn. "Halt this ship in the name of the Incorporated Planets and the Interstellar Patrol!"

Chaotica spun around and glared at Proton. "You could not have escaped my Minions!"

"Then it must be my ghost you see before you!" Proton replied with a sly grin.

The man at the weapons panel started to draw his weapon. Proton fired his ray gun, hitting the man and sending him flying over the panel.

But the other man was quick. He got off a shot at Captain Proton, just barely missing and causing Proton to duck behind a wall.

Proton fired back.

The man fired again.

"Too late, Proton!" Chaotica shouted. He moved over to the weapons panel and punched a huge button. "I have just started a giant red star on its way to your home world, Earth. Nothing can stop it!"

On the Blaster Ship's Imagizer, Proton could see that Chaotica told the truth. A beam of red shot out from the ship, directly hitting a nearby giant red star and sending it plummeting toward Earth.

Proton quickly fired his gun at the pilot's control panel, blowing it into smoke and sparks. Because of all the lights that blinked on it, he could tell that panel was the most important one in the ship. Destroy it, and the ship would lose all power.

Around the rest of the control room, panels exploded like a string of firecrackers.

Buttons, levers, and panel covers flew everywhere.

Smoke filled the control room.

Chaotica stepped back, anger and fear showing on his face. Around them the ship started to shake as if it were in an earthquake—slowly at first, then quickly building. Proton knew no ship could withstand such shaking for long.

Chaotica took a large energy pistol out of his belt and fired at Proton, just missing but exploding the panel in front of him. "You don't know what you have done!" Chaotica shouted.

Proton did know, but he didn't tell Chaotica that.

The rumbling got stronger. Now it seemed as though a giant hand had grasped the Blaster Ship and was shaking it vigorously.

Captain Proton fired back at Chaotica, sending the evil doctor scrambling for cover. "Your new ship seems to be having a problem, Doctor!" Proton shouted through the smoke. "Just how much damage did I do?" he taunted.

"Kill him!" Chaotica shouted to two other men as they entered the control room.

Then, with a flourish of his black cape, Dr. Chaotica turned and disappeared into the smoke.

Both men opened fire on Captain Proton, but he dodged their blasts and quickly knocked them out. Then he sped away to look for Chaotica. Around him, the ship kept shaking. It didn't seem as if it could hold together much longer. By destroying that panel, he had set off a chain reaction that would blow up the entire ship, just as he had planned. But he had also hoped to capture Dr. Chaotica at the same time.

He quickly searched through the corridors surrounding the control room, but he saw no sign of where the evil doctor had gone. Time was running out—capturing him would have to wait for another day. Captain Proton headed at a run for the hatch that led to his ship.

The shaking was so intense that Proton banged against walls, slipped and fell a dozen times, and tumbled head over heels twice. But finally he was out the hatch and back in his own ship.

Although his suit protected him from the extreme temperature, Proton could see right away that the heat inside his ship was almost unbearable. Buster Kincaid and Constance were soaked in sweat, their clothes stuck to their bodies, looking more like they'd been standing in a rainstorm than manning a ship. But they were very glad to see him.

"I'll take over those controls," Captain Proton ordered as he unfastened his helmet.

Kincaid stepped aside, and Proton quickly backed their ship out from between the hot jets of the Blaster Ship into the coolness of deep space.

"I didn't know if we were going to make it," Kincaid exclaimed, panting.

"I knew you could do it," Proton replied. "Watch!"

He pointed at the Imagizer as the huge Blaster Ship exploded with a massive rumble.

"Shock wave!" Proton shouted. "Hold on!"

The shock wave from the explosion tossed Proton's ship as if it were a child's toy on an ocean wave, then passed by.

"You've destroyed Chaotica's Blaster Ship!" Kincaid shouted. "Earth is saved!"

"I wish that were the case," Proton warned. He quickly adjusted the Imagizer so it showed the giant red star plummeting toward Earth. "Chaotica put his evil plan in motion before I could stop it."

"What are we going to do?" Kincaid wailed.

"We're going to save Earth," Captain Proton said, his hands holding the controls of his ship tightly. "But it may cost us our lives."

Kincaid nodded. "I'll gladly give my life to save our home planet!"

"Constance?" Proton asked, turning to his sweat-soaked secretary.

She grasped hold of a railing and nodded.

"Good," Proton said forcefully, turning back to his controls. "I knew I could count on you two one final time."

"But how can this small ship ever stop a giant red star?" Kincaid asked.

"This ship can't," Proton answered. "But the Space Vortex of Doom can."

Kincaid turned white.

Constance screamed at the very mention of the name.

Captain Proton kept his ship blasting through the ether. "We have one chance. The giant red star will pass the Space Vortex of Doom in exactly six minutes."

"But by my calculations, the giant red star will miss the Space Vortex of Doom," Kincaid said.

"I know that," Proton replied. "So we must increase the reach of the Space Vortex of Doom. The Vortex is a giant whirlpool in space, correct?"

Kincaid nodded.

"So if we dive our ship into the Space Vortex of Doom," Proton explained, "going in the same direction as the spin and accelerating, we might increase the spin and expand the reach of the Vortex."

"So it grabs the giant red star as it passes!" Kincaid exclaimed.

"Exactly!" Proton answered. "Now, man your station. I'll need you to fire all weapons straight ahead when I give the order! We'll try to give the Vortex even more energy to help it speed up!"

"Understood!" Kincaid confirmed, stepping smartly to his station.

Proton gripped the controls of his ship firmly as Kincaid's hand poised over the firing button.

On the Imagizer in front of them, the swirling black mass of the Space Vortex of Doom turned slowly, sucking down into its maw anything that strayed close. No ship, no beam of light, nothing had ever escaped the intense gravity of the Space Vortex of Doom.

Captain Proton hoped the giant red star would join that list of missing objects soon.

"We're going in!" Captain Proton shouted as the ship started to shake.

They crossed over the threshold of the Space Vortex of Doom, and the blackness of it surrounded them, swallowed them like they were in the middle of a dark night on a moonless planet.

"Full speed ahead!" Proton ordered.

Kincaid twisted the dial, giving the ship full power.

"We're moving with the spin!" Proton shouted over the roar and the shaking. "Fire all weapons straight ahead!"

"Firing!" Kincaid shouted.

Around them, the swirling blackness of the Space Vortex of Doom seemed to speed up. But there was still no sign of the giant red star.

"Fire again!" Proton ordered. "We're almost out of time!"

Kincaid did as he was told, punching the button on his panel extra hard.

Now it was clear that the blackness in motion around them had sped up.

Would it be enough to grab the giant red star?

Could they save Earth?

**150**

Captain Proton held his breath, keeping his ship moving with the current.

Buster Kincaid held his breath.

Constance Goodheart held her breath.

Suddenly the blackness around them seemed to turn a faint pink.

Then red.

Then bright red as the giant red star flashed past them and down into the depths of the Space Vortex of Doom, swirling the blackness with streaks of red.

"It worked!" Kincaid shouted.

"Yes," Proton replied. "We have saved Earth! Hold on!"

The tidal wave of Space Vortex matter smashed into them, sucking them down behind the giant red star.

No one had ever lived after coming that close to a giant red star.

No one had ever escaped from the Space Vortex of Doom.

Constance Goodheart screamed!

Captain Proton stood at the controls of his ship, fighting with all his strength to keep them from following the giant red star into the darkness below. Sweat covered his brow as the blackness swirled around them.

He was losing.

There was no escaping the Space Vortex of Doom.

Downward they spiraled.

Downward . . .

Downward . . .

Into the blackness.